I0665519

BETWEEN ROCK
AND
HARD PLACES

BETWEEN ROCK
AND
HARD PLACES
A Mike McMahon Mystery

STEPHEN METZGER

STANSBURY
PUBLISHING
Chico, Ca.

Between Rock and Hard Places
A Mike McMahon Mystery
by Stephen Metzger

Copyright © 2021 by Stephen Metzger

ISBN 978-1-635807-60-5 pbk.
ISBN 978-1-635807-61-2 ePub

Library of Congress Control Number: 2021938201
First edition

Stansbury Publishing is an imprint of
Heidelberg Graphics

All rights reserved. No part of this book maybe be reproduced
or transmitted in any form or by any means, electronic or
mechanical, including photocopying, recording, or by any
information storage and retrieval system, without permission
in writing from the copyright holders or publisher,
except for reviews.

Front cover photo of coastline © Ethan Daniels | Dreamstime.com
Front cover photo of guitar © Jaroslaw Grudzinski | Dreamstime.com

Jim Rooney's maroon 1965 Mustang convertible sailed off High-way 1 just north of San Francisco a little after 10:00 one morning last February, crashing twenty feet below into boulders and foamy Pacific whitewater. According to the *Independent Journal*, the lo-cal newspaper, and a brief obit in *Rolling Stone*, he'd gone into cardiac arrest and lost consciousness and probably didn't even know he'd left the road. His widow wasn't so sure. She thought he might have been murdered.

She'd been waiting for me when I got out of class.

I'm a private investigator but to make ends meet, I teach a course at Marin Community College in the history of rock 'n' roll. A lot of the kids who sign up think they're going to get to lis-ten to Led Zeppelin and watch YouTube clips for homework, and then drop the second week when I assign Rimbaud, Ginsberg, and Frederick Douglass, and tell them that we'll be studying Brown vs. Board of Education and that anyone who calls Jim Morrison a poet automatically fails. Not that I don't take full advantage of the miracle of YouTube.

"Mr. McMahon?"

She looked too old to be a student and too alert to be an administrator.

"Uh huh."

"My name's Sarah Rooney. My husband used to play with the Johnny Sands Band."

I stopped short, although I'd have been glad for any distraction.

Shelley Martin had followed me out of class wanting me to read a draft of her paper on women's music of the '60s and '70s. "Why don't you work a bit more on narrowing your topic?" I said. "We'll take a look at it next week." She nodded, and Mrs. Rooney and I watched her walk away.

"I'm sorry," she said. "I know you're a very busy man, but I need your help. Can I buy you a cup of coffee? Or something else?"

A glass of something else sounded really, really good. I looked at my watch.

"Stronger?"

"You know the Owl Cafe?" I said.

"Sure."

"Meet you there in fifteen minutes."

I stopped by the department office to check my email, hoping maybe there was a note from Bruce inviting me to go on tour with him. Nope. Not yet. I headed across campus to the Owl. It was early April and there was already a pleasant warmth in the air.

The Owl is a classic old-Marin bar with a storied past. The Irish playwright Brendan Behan used to show up in the early 1960s after escaping from San Francisco, where he was supposed to be drying out. Some say a one-night stand with a woman he met there produced his only son. In the late 1960s and early '70s, regulars included Van Morrison, John Cippolina, Elvin Bishop, Huey Lewis, and David Crosby. Their black-and-white photos, many of them signed, are scattered crookedly on the dark wooden walls.

Mrs. Rooney was already sitting at a stool at the bar when

I walked in, her denim skirt hiked up, one leg crossed narrowly over the other. Though her hair was streaked with gray and her face lined and leathered, she was still a very attractive woman. Sixty, sixty-five, I figured. She wore a loose-fitting embroidered tank top tucked into her skirt, Birkenstock sandals, and turquoise earrings, which accented her pale blue eyes. The skin on her upper chest was pale and smooth, lightly mottled. She wore several rings on each hand.

I sat down beside her, and she turned to me. She had a glass of something else on the rocks in front of her. Impressive.

"Thanks for coming," she said.

I nodded at the woman tending bar, who poured a Jameson's over and set it in front of me.

"I was sorry to hear about Jim," I said. "I'm a huge fan. Wish I'd been around in the old days."

She took a long deep breath and sipped at her drink.

"Sorry," I said. "That's probably the last thing you want to talk about."

She looked up, shook her head. "No, that's exactly what I want to talk about."

I took a sip of my whiskey and waited for her to continue.

"You saw the papers. Jimmy goes into cardiac arrest, his car goes off the road, he dies. Pretty straightforward, right?"

"I guess."

"Well, it wasn't like that. I mean obviously his car did go off the road, and obviously he did die. But I'm convinced he . . . " She trailed off.

I looked up suddenly.

She shook her head slowly. "The thing is, Jimmy had had

3

some heart issues. A-Fib about five years ago, but he'd been treated and was on meds and doing fine. Perfect health."

"But, Mrs. Rooney, a lot of guys seem to be in perfect health, and then . . . " I didn't know how to end the sentence I'd started.

"I know," she said. "And if the circumstances were different, I'd say fine, he went into cardiac arrest, whatever, naturally, and I'd be good with that." She had emphasized the word "naturally."

I looked at her skeptically. "You don't think his death was . . . natural?"

She shook her head, deliberately.

"You think he was murdered?"

She took another long breath, bit her lower lip, then nodded.

"I'm sorry, Mrs.—"

"Sarah."

"—Sarah . . . I'm sorry, but I don't quite follow. Wasn't there a coroner's report?"

"Sure, and that's where the cardiac-arrest stuff came from. But it was pure speculation."

"I'm not sure I follow you," I said.

She took a deep breath. "I regret it now," she said, "but I didn't have them do an autopsy."

"So, they just *assumed* it was cardiac arrest? And then that caused the crash?"

"Well, it would be a natural assumption," she said. "He'd been treated for the heart condition and everything." She shook her head. "In fact, it's how his father died. So, if you didn't have any reason not to, you'd just say cardiac arrest."

4

"You have a reason not to?"

She nodded, then held her empty glass up to the bartender. "Look," she said. "Jimmy was writing a book. In fact, he'd finished the book."

"A book?" I have a knack for the brilliant response.

The bartender replaced her glass with another and poured a couple of shots of Jameson's over the rocks.

I drained mine and held the empty glass up for a refill.

"Great minds . . . " she said, then to the bartender. "Thank you." She forced a smile, then turned back to me. "About his days with Johnny Sands, and the band. About the early days. Everything, in fact. The plane crash. Afterwards."

"Not to doubt your word, Mrs., uh, Sarah, but who would want to kill him to keep him from writing a book?"

"That's what I need you for."

I sipped my whiskey. "Let's back up for a second. You say you don't have anything concrete that he was murdered. What do you have that makes you think that his death was connected to what he was writing?"

"It's what I don't have," she said.

"What you don't have?"

"The book."

"You don't have the book?" Another impressive *bon mot*.

"The morning he died, he was on his way to the post office to mail the back-up hard copy to his publisher. He'd gotten up early, written his acknowledgments, and then he woke me up and took me to breakfast. Afterward, he dropped me off at home, put the manuscript in a box, and headed out. We, I mean I, live out by Pt. Reyes Station, and he said he had some other errands to run in San Rafael. He said he was going to email the final files when he got home that afternoon. I'd never seen him so happy as when he pulled out of the driveway. Of course with his Mustang's top down. He waved the box with the manuscript in it, blew me a kiss, and that was the last time I saw him alive."

"I still don't get it," I said. "What happened to the book?"

"Gone," she said. "Wasn't in his car when they found him. Or at least, it wasn't among his 'personal effects' that the cops brought back to the house."

A kid in a John Lennon t-shirt and a backwards baseball cap pulled a stool up onto the tiny stage in the corner, set his open guitar case in front of him, and began to tune. I thought about offering him twenty bucks not to play.

"Didn't his agent, or his publisher, someone, have a copy, of at least part of it?"

"Agent?" She smiled softly and shook her head. "He'd written to the publisher directly and they gave him the go-ahead. Based on what he knew and his connections. I assumed they planned to rewrite it pretty extensively." She smiled again. "I think he thought they'd publish it exactly as he wrote it."

"Surely you've got the files, a draft . . . something. I didn't think publishers even *wanted* hard copy anymore."

"I know," she said. "But he'd gotten an email a couple of weeks before asking him to send the actual manuscript. Seems strange to me now."

"But what about electronic files? His computer?"

She shook her head. "I had to go down to the coroner's office to identify the body. Horrible. Really. I stayed that night with my sister, and then went back to the house in the morning.

I'm a strong woman, Mr. McMahon. I was going to be fine." She paused. She didn't seem all that strong right then. "When I got back to the house, I went straight to Jimmy's office. I needed a distraction, wanted to figure out right away what needed to be done. You should have seen the place. Papers everywhere. Files all over the floor. A mess."

"Someone had broken in?" That's why they pay me the big bucks.

She nodded, sipping her drink. "And taken his computer. A little laptop I'd bought him when he'd first gotten serious about the book."

I let out a soft whistle, just like a good P.I. is supposed to. "I see what you mean. I assume you called the police."

She smiled. "Sure. And they came out. Robbery, they said. I guess computers are big these days on the hot market. Cops say they get ripped off all the time."

"You tell them about the book Jimmy was writing?"

"I started to, but they didn't seem interested. Coming out at all seemed like a chore to them."

I nodded.

"Mr. McMahon, Jimmy was a good man. I don't know what all was in that book—he wasn't going to let me see it until it was published—but he was proud of it. He was also a very honest man. Stubbornly so. I'm sure he wrote about some things that people from those days wouldn't want the public to know. It's been glossed over. Those were strange times."

"But could there really be anything that terrible? So incriminating that someone would rather see him dead than see the book get published?"

7

She shrugged. "I honestly don't know. But I can't move on until I at least know more. Know something."

"Was he getting any money from the songs?" I asked.

She shook her head. "A tiny bit. He was their drummer. Johnny wrote all the songs. That's where the money went, or should have. I really don't know." She set her glass down. Two Irish whiskeys in a half hour. She looked at me. "Mr. McMahon, will you help me find out who killed my husband?"

I reached for my wallet, but she put her hand on my arm and slipped a $20 bill under her glass.

"Let me think about it," I said. "Here's my card. Today's Monday, call me at home Wednesday."

"Mr. McMahon—"

"Mike."

"Mike . . . I can pay you whatever you charge. Jimmy didn't make out as well as some of the musicians, but we got by."

I nodded. "Oh, one more thing? Who was the publisher? I'd like to talk to them, see if they have anything at all."

"Narwhal Books," she said. "I think they're out of Seattle. But really, I don't think he communicated much with them after they said they were interested in looking at it."

"You never know," I said.

She nodded. "I'll call you Wednesday." She stood up, shook my hand and thanked me again, and disappeared through the door out onto the street.

I ordered another whiskey, stood, and fished in my pocket for some quarters. John Lennon was still trying to tune his guitar. I walked over to him. "You mind?" I said, indicating the jukebox.

"Guess not," he said. I walked over, flipped through the songs, and put on some Johnny Sands. Also some Kinks and Merle Haggard.

— 2 —

The Johnny Sands Band was one of the country's most popular rock 'n' roll bands of the mid-1970s. Real country boys from backwoods North Carolina playing scorching southern rock *a la* Lynyrd Skynryd and the Allman Brothers, mixed in with some genuinely powerful ballads and softer Marshall Tucker-type love songs. Johnny Sands was one of those rare musicians. Brilliant songwriter and singer—and with the good looks and the stage presence that sold records and concert tickets. They only recorded for a few years but in that time had several FM hits, one AM cross-over, and three albums that musicians to this day credit with being major influences on their careers. Of course, there are a handful of Johnny Sands tribute bands out there today playing county fairs and casinos. One from southern California is called the Sands Diegos.

When I got home it was 10:30. I put on the first Johnny Sands CD, *Time of Sands*, and went out onto the back porch and rubbed Luther's belly, then let him rest his head in my lap as I watched the moon go down behind Mt. Tam. I hadn't run him that day, and I could tell by the look in his eyes that he was not a happy camper. Dogs need exercise, and smart dogs know that you know that. Newfoundland retrievers—especially Luther—have a way just by looking at you of making you feel guilty for not devoting your entire life to them.

Which, honestly, wouldn't be hard for me to do.

As I was promising Luther a run on the beach tomorrow, my phone buzzed. It was Becka. Ah, Becka. Rebecca Goldberg. Professor of English at San Francisco State, specializing in Anglo-Saxon literature. Old San Francisco family with lots of money. Homes at Sea Cliff, Carmel, and Tahoe. Smart, funny, and both headstrong and full of charm—like her father, Dr. Simon Goldberg, Stanford Medical School anesthesiologist, author, philanthropist.

We met four years ago in a Chinese-cooking class. We got together for a drink in Sausalito the afternoon before the final meeting and then ended up back at my place. Never even made it to that last class. She stayed for four days. We left my house only for short visits to the market or to the take-out place on the corner for Mu Goo Gai Pan. I gave her an "A."

Things were great at first, but for the past three years it might as well have been our picture next to the word "dysfunctional" in the textbook for a psychology-of-love-and-marriage class.

"What're you doin'?" she said.

"Just listening to some music."

"Want to come over? I got a pint of Cherry Garcia ice cream, and I'm all alone."

"Uh . . . not this time."

"Suit yourself. More for me."

"Hey, Beck. You remember the Johnny Sands Band?"

"You and your classic rock. Way before my time."

"Oh that's right. I should have asked you if you remember

Justin Timberlake."

"Actually," she said. "I like some of those old songs. 'Hannah Lou.'"

"Great song."

"Didn't Johnny Sands die in a plane crash or something?"

"Yep, after a concert one night."

We talked for a few more minutes.

"When will we see each other?"

"I don't know," I said. "Not tomorrow, and probably not the day after. I gotta work."

"Fine."

I could tell she was angry when she hung up. I went back in the house and picked up the CD jewel box and stood looking at the cover for a minute. There were four musicians in the band: Johnny; his brother Kevin, who played guitar; the bass player, Lester Corbin; and Jimmy Rooney. They looked like kids, which I guess they were, posed there on the front porch of some shack in the woods somewhere. Kevin, Jim Rooney, and Corbin all scraggily bearded and overalled, Corbin holding a jug of moonshine. Johnny sat cross-legged on the weathered wooden steps in front of them, hugging his knees into his chest, in cowboy boots, jeans, and a leather jacket, his long dark hair falling down and hiding most of his face.

I went over to my computer and Googled Johnny Sands. If you're careful, Wikipedia can be a godsend. Johnny and Kevin were the sons of Don Sands, cotton farmer and champion fiddle player from Raleigh, North Carolina, who died when the boys were very young. Their mother, who'd played organ and sung in church choirs, started them playing music almost before they could walk, and the boys, along with their younger sister, Doreen, were performing as the Sand Tunes before they reached high school. Kevin met Corbin and Rooney when they played high school football together. When *Time of Sands* was released, Corbin, Rooney, and Kevin Sands were 20. Johnny was 18. Doreen died when she was 29, and Kevin's battled mental-health issues most of his life and was still living in a care facility somewhere here in northern California. The band's manager was a former disc jockey named Howard Silva.

I picked up the jewel box and turned it over in my hands. What a shame. Doreen dead. Johnny dead in a plane crash. Kevin institutionalized. And now Jimmy Rooney dead. Maybe murdered. I wondered what ever happened to Corbin. I went to Youtube and found a live "Hannah Lou" from an outdoor concert in 1974. Really crappy footage but I sang along:

Oh my Hannah Lou, won't you move up to the country
Hold my hand and walk along the river with me

Not great lyrics by any stretch of the imagination—or even among Johnny's best, which were often full of puns and wordplay—but there was something about the way Johnny sang them, so honestly and selflessly, the words weaving in and out of and all around Kevin's plaintive bottleneck, that it became a truly great song

Becka called back a little after 11. "Look," she said. "I'm sorry. Did I sound mean?"

"Nah." I hit Speaker on the phone, set it on the counter, and reached for the second Johnny Sands CD.

"Anyway, I'm sorry. I know you're busy and all."

"It's okay."

"Mike?"

"Yeah?"

"Can I come over? I looked at my watch.

"Mike?"

"I thought you taught in the morning."

"I do, but I just finished reading a batch of papers on *Beow-ulf,* I'm all ready for my class, and I can't really sleep."

"Got any of that ice cream left?"

"Asshole."

"I'm serious. I'll let you come over and have sex with me if you bring me some ice cream."

"Asshole," she said again and hung up.

She was at my door in fifteen minutes.

No ice cream.

So what.

— 3 —

Johnny Sands' plane went down on July 16, 1976. He was 23. The band had just played a concert in Albuquerque, and his little Cessna slammed into the side of the Sandia Mountains a half hour after take-off. There's never been a convincing case for what caused the crash.

He was the only band member on board—just him and the pilot—on his way home to Raleigh between gigs. Instead, his body was flown back two days later, and there was a private burial and then a public service. The rest of the tour was canceled. The other three never played together again.

Johnny Sands' gravesite in Raleigh has become a sort of shrine, with kids from all over the world stopping by to lay plastic flowers, scrap-paper poems, beer bottles, and all kinds of crap next to the headstone. Of course, every now and again, usually around his birthday, the rumors that he didn't really die start up again.

I was vaguely aware of Becka's getting out of bed, and she was showered and gone by the time I got up at 9:30. I went to the stereo, ejected the Johnny Sands CD and put on *Astral Weeks*, Van Morrison's early masterpiece. There was a note from Becka on the counter that she'd fed Luther. I made myself a cup of coffee and called Sarah Rooney.

"I hope I'm not calling too early."

"No, I've been up for hours. I hope I wasn't too, well, you know, intense yesterday, it's just that I—"

"I understand."

"Then you're going to help?"

"I'm not sure yet."

She didn't say anything.

"Sarah, tell me about Kevin?"

I could hear her take a breath. "Poor kid. I'm sure you've read about him. I don't know what put him over. Some say it was drugs, but I don't know. He had a good head on his shoulders." She paused. "He lives up in the wine country. Vineland Group Home."

"Why out here?" I said. "Northern California. It's a long way from Releigh?"

"I guess they wanted to set him up in a completely different environment. Clear his head."

"When did . . . ?"

"Apparently not long after the crash. Jimmy said he started acting really weird. Then just disappeared one day. Something about finding him sitting on some beach, crosslegged and staring out at the water. Like he'd been there for days. I don't know the whole story."

"You or Jimmy ever see him?"

"Jimmy went up a couple of times, but it was really hard on him. He always talked about going back but never did. Their mom goes out from time to time."

"Whatever happened to her?"

"Connie? Living in Phoenix as far as I know."

"She'd have to be, what—? Eighty?"

"Something like that. I guess she got remarried, and then divorced. Living alone down there."

"You know what she goes by?"

"I'm pretty sure she kept her name. The guy she married was named . . . Larry Grant."

"You know anything about him?"

"Not really."

"Sarah, didn't Johnny have a kid?"

She was silent.

I waited.

"Yes. Just after their second album came out. Roger. Carla was the gal's name. They were supposed to get married."

"Where's she now?"

"Down south. Somewhere, out in the desert, I think."

"And the kid, Roger?"

"Jimmy told me he was trying to make it as a musician in L.A."

"He must be getting a pretty decent chunk of those residuals."

"Apparently, there were some restrictions on the money. I guess he's getting a little bit . . . Like I told you, Jimmy sure never saw much of it."

"Whatever happened to Lester Corbin?"

"Lester? He kept playing music for a while. Moved out to L.A. and did some studio work. Got married, had a couple of kids. Pretty normal, I think. He and his wife moved out to Santa Fe twenty or so years ago and bought a bed and breakfast. We never really saw him. Except once or twice when they passed through on vacation. We still get Christmas cards from them."

We talked for a few more minutes. By the time I hung up, I was trying to figure out where to start on the Jimmy Rooney case, although I realized I already had.

— 4 —

I've had a private practice for nearly ten years now. I played guitar in rock 'n' roll bands to put myself through college, getting my undergraduate and master's degrees in American history from U.C. Berkeley—my thesis was about Stephen Foster's influence on the early '60s Greenwich Village folk scene—and then played music around the San Francisco Bay Area for a while, thinking that any day I'd get that big break. Never did, though I like to think I've still got my chops.

I thought for a while about going to graduate school for a Ph.D., but I realized the price was too high. I was terrified that I'd have had to buy a Volvo station wagon and a pair of Crocs. Thankfully, I took a handful of criminal justice courses, which made it much easier to get my P.I. license—which came with a gun permit so I didn't have to apply for concealed carry.

Not that I take much advantage of that. In fact, I conceal my Smith and Wesson in a locked drawer in my nightstand. Never felt much need to haul it around. And never wished I had it on me. Knock on wood.

Though Becka did talk me into hiring a home-security company last year. Very bare bones. No fancy cameras, just an alarm system. If it ever gets triggered, the company's supposed to call me. If I don't answer, they call the cops. I guess it makes sense in my line of work and living on a little dead-end street in the woods, my only nearby neighbor the hippie-chick in the cottage down my driveway across the road. Raven.

My rock 'n' roll class only meets once a week, Monday, so I still had six days to prepare for my lecture. Piece of cake. The British invasion. I always liked telling the class I was going to be talking about the Brits—Rod Stewart, Jeff Beck, the Beatles and Stones—and then playing Black American blues pioneers like Charlie Patton, Son House, and Robert Johnson, as well as Howlin' Wolf and Bo Diddly.

I burned the three Johnny Sands CDs onto my iTunes and reloaded my iPod. Then I loaded Luther into the back of my pick-up, and headed out to Fort Cronkite. There are a lot of beaches in California, but not too many welcome 150-pound Newfoundland retrievers. Fort Cronkite was cool, though. I just had to make sure I brought along a couple of large plastic bags.

When we got to the beach, I let Luther out and jogged down to the water. The tide was low, and there was hardly anyone out. A crisp wind swirled the fog along the cliffs and up around the bunkers and over the Marine Mammal Center. I threw a couple of sticks for Luther, then let him entertain himself in the waves while I listened to Johnny Sands on my iPod.

One of the trademarks of the Johnny Sands Band was the little guitar hook at the beginning of each song. I always figured that that was Kevin saying, *Look, I'm here too.* It must have been difficult to be in Johnny's shadow all the time, though Johnny always made plenty of room for him.

The second Johnny Sands album, *Sandy Morning,* was the one that put the band in the public eye. There were four or five really great songs, all written by Johnny, that you still hear today on Spotify and Pandora. "Since Gina Told Danny Good-bye," "Out on a Limb," "Send for the Jester," "Your Love," "Forever and Today." All great songs, lots of them covered by scores of other second-rate bands. In fact, I heard "Since Gina Told Danny Good-bye" in the grocery store the other day with about a million strings. Or probably one synthesizer.

Sarah Rooney called as we were heading back to Mill Valley. One of those times I wished I'd installed Bluetooth on my truck so I could take her call without holding my phone. I let her leave a voice mail and called her back when I got home.

"Oh, Mike. I was hoping that would be you. Can you meet me? I need to talk to you."

"Sure. When?"

"This evening," she said. "I'll buy dinner."

Couldn't argue with that.

"How 'bout the Grotto? Six-thirty?"

"See you there."

I spent the afternoon doing a bit of work on my pick-up, a 1972 Chevy Cheyenne 10 long-bed that I found in barn up in Butte County outside of Chico. It was pretty beat, but the body was straight, and I've spent the last couple of years restoring it, trying to use as many all-original parts as I can. Just a couple of weeks earlier, I'd found a nearly perfect steering wheel on eBay—Buy Now for $220!—so I installed that. Then I did a bit of sanding on some bodywork I'd done on the left rear quarter panel and primed it. It was starting to look pretty good. I figured I'd have it ready to paint by mid-summer. I hated having the camper shell on it, but it was the only way to get Luther around, though he much preferred riding shotgun with me in the cab.

Around five, I showered, dressed, and headed down to the Grotto, where the maître d' asked if I was Mr. McMahon, then showed me to a table where Sarah was waiting.

"Thanks for coming," she said.

I had barely sat down when a waiter appeared, looking annoyed. "My name is Antoine," he said. He had a pierced eyebrow and some Asian characters tattooed up one forearm and a full-on paragraph in tiny font on the other. "I'll be your server this evening." Indeed. He told us about a couple of specials, sturgeon baked in a Dijon sauce and grilled quail, then said, "Can I start you off with something to drink?"

I ordered a Sierra Nevada Pale Ale, of which Antoine clearly did not approve, and Sarah ordered a Jameson's on the rocks. "Old habits," she said, smiling.

I shrugged. "They die hard."

She smiled again, then quickly looked serious. "I'm sorry, Mike, I know you said to wait until tomorrow to call you, but I got a phone call today that I thought might interest you."

Antoine reappeared with our drinks. I took a big slug of my ale.

"Really," I said, wiping the beer foam from my upper lip with a napkin. "From . . . ?"

"Roger Sands."

"No kidding."

"I saw him at Jimmy's memorial service," she said, "but we never got the chance to chat. He's living in Los Angeles, has been for the past five or six years. He says he's about to land a 'major recording contract.'" She made quote marks in the air with her fingers.

"You don't believe him?"

"I don't know. I mean, I should I guess . . . "

"Is that what he was calling you about?"

"I'm not sure. It was very strange. He was kind of round-about for a long time, just sort of gabbing away like we were old friends that needed to get caught up, and then just as he was about to hang up, he asked me if I knew how to get a hold of Lester Corbin."

"Corbin?"

"Yeah, weird, huh?"

"Did he say what he wanted to talk to him about?"

"No. He did leave me a phone number, though."

Antoine appeared, looking as if he were doing us a favor. I asked him to tell me again about the sturgeon, then ordered the swordfish. Sarah ordered the scampi. "Very well," he said and turned to the kitchen.

"Oh, and I'd like another beer," I said after him.

He stopped without turning, took a visible breath, then continued walking away.

I looked at Sarah Rooney. "I know I asked you not to call me until Wednesday, but I should tell you I'm very interested in this case. I was a big fan of the Johnny Sands Band, and of your husband's. I've got most of those jazz albums he did in the eighties."

Sarah smiled and took a sip of her drink. "That's how he ended up out here. Followed Lester Corbin out to LA, and they worked in the studios together for a while. He made those jazz records on the side. That's when we met. I was doing freelance graphic design and he needed an album cover."

"Sounds like a fairytale," I said.

"Kinda was. We went out for six months then drove to Reno and got married. He kept playing music, and I kept drawing pictures. Finally, we couldn't take LA anymore, retired, and moved up here to Marin five years ago."

"Kids?"

She shook her head. "Just the two of us."

"I'll need a thousand up front," I said. "That, plus expenses, will cover two weeks. After that, we'll see where we stand."

"Oh, Mike. I can't thank you enough."

"Don't thank me yet."

Antoine showed up with our orders. I told him I'd changed my mind and wanted the sturgeon after all.

— 5 —

I figured I ought to begin with the law.

My first thought was my buddy Denny Kenkel at the Mill Valley P.D. We'd worked on several cases together and he always had my back. This was clearly a case for the sheriff's office, though, the accident having occurred in the county's jurisdiction.

Marin County Deputy Sheriff Stan Harper and I went to Drake High School together. He was a couple of years ahead of me, but I knew who he was and over the last few years have taken advantage of our having an alma mater in common. Actually, almost everyone knew who he was—as a running back on the football team he broke just about every record in the school's history.

As I drove up the hill to Harper's office in the Hall of Justice in the Marin County Civic Center, I was impressed, as I always was no matter how many times I'd seen it, which is hundreds. A huge, L-shaped, blue-domed building blending into the hillside beside Highway 101, just north of San Rafael, it was the last design commissioned by Frank Lloyd Wright in 1957 and completed in 1969, a year before Black Panther Jonathan Jackson, Judge Harold Haley, and two others were killed in an attempted jail break in the parking lot.

Some people pay to tour places Wright designed. I knew guys who got the tour of this one free. Of course, it cost them later in lawyer fees. And car-insurance premiums. And time off from work for AA meetings.

Harper's secretary waved me into his office, where he was sitting behind his desk at a computer. He still looked like he could play football. Thick forearms, broad shoulders, and a strong neck. His hair had thinned a bit, but he could have passed for ten years younger. His country-green short-sleeved shirt pulled tight across his chest, the badge catching a hint of the overhead light. I stood in the doorway for several seconds before he finally looked up.

"Hey, McMahon, what're you up to?" He looked back to the computer screen, then moved the mouse, and clicked. "Long time no see. Sit down."

I nodded, and sat down in the round-backed oak chair beside his desk.

He got up and closed the door behind me, then sat back down. I looked at the photos on the wall—Harper in waders beside a stream holding a silvery steelhead, Harper in a field kneeling beside a yellow Lab with a pheasant in its mouth, Harper standing atop Half Dome in Yosemite. "Let's see, last I heard you were, what, doing espionage for cuckolds?" He laughed.

"Something like that."

"You still playing music?"

I shook my head. "Not as much as I'd like to."

"Well, what's up, man? Seems like the only times I see you are when you want something. Or over at the gym."

"You remember when Jim Rooney died?"

"Sure, had a heart attack and crashed out on Highway 1. Why?"

"Cardiac arrest," I said.

"Right."

"His widow's not so sure it was an accident."

Harper scoffed. "Come on, man. The old pumper gave out, he missed the turn and got big air off the highway. Dude's a regular Thelma and Louise. Plus, he was driving that old Mustang. Those things were built a thousand years before airbags. What's she think, he got run off the road?"

I shrugged. "She doesn't think it was his heart."

He scowled, then shook his head. "What? Some *bad guy* cut his brake cables? Only happens on television, Mike."

"Ah, I don't know. She's probably crazy."

"What's she got?"

I didn't want to go into it with him, at least not yet. "Just that I guess he was the picture of health."

"Come on, Mike, you know as well as I do that guys younger than him drop dead on treadmills and basketball courts all the time. You never know." He stood and went to the window, looked down on the lagoon below.

I shrugged. "What are the chances of taking a look at the coroner's report?"

"I can get you a copy."

Harper turned and reached for his phone, ordered the copy, then put his hand over the phone. "They can get me hard copy. You want to come by and pick it up?"

"Sure."

"Yeah, just send it up here."

I stood to leave, thanked him, and was about to reach for the door. Harper stood, opened the door for me, then put his hand on my shoulder. "You know," he said, "I just thought of something. I didn't think it meant much at the time, but . . . . "

"What?"

"The only witness to the accident—ranch hand named Rodriguez, working out on the Ginanelli place—said a car stopped right afterward, and someone got out, and went over to the cliffside. Rodriguez was the one who called 911. Said he figured the guy was going down to the water to see if he could do anything but that he climbed back and drove away."

"Rodriguez?"

"Pedro. We never followed up, what with it being cardiac arrest and all. Didn't seem like anything."

"Probably wasn't."

"Probably."

"Thanks," I said, "and thanks for getting me the copy of the report."

"You bet," he said, then, "Hey, McMahon. You playing any round ball these days?"

"Some."

"Looking good, man."

I nodded.

"You thirty yet?"

"Thirty-one," I said.

I was accumulating quite a list of people to talk to. Lester Corbin. Roger Sands. Maybe Kevin. And now Rodriguez. That seemed the next logical step.

I looked at my watch. Not even noon. I drove home and fired up my little 1963 356 "bathtub" Porsche, which I "acquired," you might say, when a client couldn't pay his bill. When I first picked it up, it needed a whole lot of work, but I pulled the engine, rebuilt it, and had the interior and bodywork done. It's gorgeous. Off-white. Cabriolet. I've gotten it up to 100, but it'll go much faster. Perfect for afternoon drives out to the coast. Becka came up with the name, "Portia"—which she had to explain to me.

I'd passed the Gianelli ranch dozens of times. As a kid with my folks on weekend picnic trips, and then two or three times a week my senior year in high school when Laurie'd climb on the back of my Honda 350 Super Sport and we'd ride out to the coast. The Gianellis were one of the original dairy families in west Marin, and they've held out. I'd gone to school with one of the Gianelli brothers. Nice kid. Our teachers used to to give him a hard time about his boots always smelling like cowshit but it never bothered me.

I took the long way, out Lucas Valley Road, through Nicasio, and then out past the lake. The water was high, and a strong northwest wind white-capped the surface. I remembered as a kid all the hours I spent fishing for largemouth bass from the banks. I also thought about George Lucas filming the drag-race scene from *American Graffiti* out on these flats. Inspiring. Got her up to 95. Briefly. Very briefly.

The Gianelli spread was 300 acres or so, with three large barns, two small houses, and the large main house, all tucked in a little valley about two hundred yards off the road, partially hidden behind a row of ancient eucalyptus trees. I parked on the shoulder and walked toward the main cluster of buildings.

I knocked on the door of the main house. A woman in a calico dress and apron answered, looking like she'd just stepped off the set of the Italian version of *The Waltons*. I wondered where

Giovanni Boy was. "Yes?"

"Hi . . . Mrs. Gianelli?"

"Yes?" She was guarded.

"My name's Mike McMahon. I knew Pete in high school."

She nodded.

"I'm looking for Mr. Rodriguez."

She looked down, twirling her apron in her fingers, then looked across the field, as though for help.

"I understand he works for you."

"Did."

"Did?"

She nodded. "Quit."

"He say where he was going?"

"He didn't say anything. Just didn't show up for work one day. We thought he was just sick, or maybe had family troubles—he had a wife and three or four kids—but he just never came back." She was in her late forties, I'd guess, probably never been out of the county, maybe never off the farm. She had long wavy salt-and-pepper hair held back in a tight bun, some of it tumbling out rebelliously, sharp features, high cheekbones, and deep-set dark eyes. Her hands looked strong. "What did you want to talk to him about?"

"I heard his wife was a good cook. I have a catering business. When was the last time you saw him?"

She looked at her watch as if out of habit, then said, "Oh, it's been, what, a week? I assume he's gone back to Mexico. That's usually what it is when they disappear like that. Definitely didn't leave for a better job here in Marin. He wasn't going to get better work than what we had for him."

I thanked her and walked back out to the road, then drove toward the coast, heading south past Stinson, pulling over for a few minutes where Rooney's Mustang had sailed off the cliff. Then I drove back up over Mount Tam, slid back into the garage, warmed up some Red Boy pizza, ate a couple of slices, and took Luther for a long walk.

— 6 —

When Luther and I got back from our walk, I polished off the pizza, washing it down with a Pale Ale, then showered. When I got out I had a missed call from Becka, with a message. "Mike, I had a hellacious department meeting today. I need to talk to somebody sane. Call me, okay?" There was a pause. "Just not late for dinner."

I fed Luther instead.

Then I went to Allmusic.com and read up on the Johnny Sands Band's manager Howard Silva, who, it turns out, had used his on-air name, R.C. Memphis, until the second album put the band in the spotlight.

Apparently, Johnny took a one-song demo tape down to the radio station where Silva was working. Silva wasn't all that impressed by Johnny's song, but told him he'd play it over the air and see what kind of response it got. The phones rang off the hook, with listeners wanting more, and Silva decided then and there to represent the band.

His first move was to get the band to cut another demo tape, with enough songs to show their range of material. They had four original tunes. Silva wanted eight. That meant that Johnny and Kevin had to get to work. Johnny showed up a week later with four new songs. They went into the studio, and Silva started shopping the tape around. He also started getting them gigs. And more than just high-school dances. Before long, the Johnny Sands Band was playing county fairs, battles of the bands around the state, and even appearing on a local television station, which was owned by Silva's brother-in-law. They cut their first album about six months later.

Silva booked all the Johnny Sands Band concerts, arriving in town a day or so before each show to check the venue, assess ticket sales, and set up sound checks. Then he'd watch the shows from the wings.

In the morning I called Sarah Rooney and asked her to meet me for coffee.

"Grounds Hero in Sausalito?" she asked.

"Perfect."

I decided to take Luther and swing by the beach afterward. I dropped the tailgate, he hopped in, and I headed into Sausalito and found a parking spot right on Bridgeway, right in front of the coffee shop. I ordered a double espresso and sat back to read the *Chronicle* while I waited for Sarah, flipping first to sports.

"Nice win last night."

I looked up.

Sarah was standing beside the table. She wore blue jeans and a yellow silk blouse. Her hair was pulled back into a ponytail.

I put the paper down, pulled a chair out, and she slid into it.

"Nice they finally got some pitching," she said.

"No kiddin'." I said. "You order?"

29

She nodded. "Just a latte and fruit salad."

Her coffee and fruit came, and I told her about what Harper had said, and then about talking to Mrs. Gianelli. Sarah didn't seem surprised.

"You think you'll be able to find Rodriguez?"

"I doubt it. If this is really what you say it is, then he's long gone."

"Gone?"

"Probably got paid enough to go back to Mexico. Or wherever. El Salvador. Wife, kids, aunts, uncles . . . his whole home town."

Sarah took a sip of her latte.

I asked her if she knew what happened to Howard Silva.

She shook her head. "No idea."

"Kinda odd that he'd just disappear after being so much a part of the band's success."

She shrugged. "Maybe. But the band was done. He probably moved on to greener pastures."

The espresso was kicking in, and I started thinking ahead of myself.

"Sarah, let me ask you a question."

"Go ahead."

"The Johnny Sands Band had some hits, they sold a lot of albums, their songs are everywhere. Glen Campbell and Justin Bieber covered 'Hannah Lou' and I hear it in the grocery store."

"I know."

I wiped my mouth with a napkin. "Where's all that money going?"

"Well, some goes to pay for Kevin's care, I guess."

"Seems that it'd take a fraction of what those songs are earning."

She shrugged.

"He completely dependent?"

"Might as well be. Chronic schizophrenic. I guess he goes out from time to time, but not without an attendant. They just can't leave him to his own devices. He'd walk in front of a bus or something. Those places are expensive." She twirled one of her hoop earrings.

"Can you think of anything else that someone from the old days with the band would want to hide? Did your husband ever tell you anything at all that someone—anyone—wouldn't want to be public knowledge?"

She let her eyelids fall, then put her hand to her forehead and ran it back through her hair. "Mike . . . I've racked my brain trying to remember everything Jimmy told me about the old days. They partied a lot, but everyone did back then. God, even George Bush and Clinton smoked pot."

"But Clinton didn't inhale."

She laughed. "I can't think of anything at all. Really. Nothing."

I nodded. "Well, if you think of anything, call me, okay?"

Luther was ecstatic to see me when I returned to the truck. "Sorry, boy," I said, scratching his snout.

We headed out to Fort Cronkite, and I let him run for a long time on the beach. On the way back to Mill Valley, he lay down in the bed of the pick-up and dozed the whole way, something he rarely does.

When I got home, I Googled Howard Silva. Odd, except

for the Allmusic article, there was nothing, except for some obviously other Howard Silvas. He seemed to have simply disappeared.

— 7 —

Harper called shortly after 9:00 Friday morning. Pedro Rodriguez had been found the day before face down in the San Rafael canal, not far from Terrapin Crossroads, a little restaurant/night club owned and managed by Phil Lesh, the Grateful Dead's bass player. The incoming tide was bumping his bloated body up against a rotting pier.

"Bummer, huh?" Harper said. "Apparently he was a hard worker, family man. Shared an apartment in the Canal with another family. Eight or nine of them, I think. Little two-bedroom place."

"What else do you know about him?" I said.

That's about it." Then, "Hey, got that coroner's report. It's sitting right here on my desk."

"'Thanks. Any chance of getting the address of that place in the Canal?"

"I don't see why not. Public information. I'll set it on the counter."

I hung up, drove over to the courthouse, picked up the copy of Jimmy Rooney's coroner's report. There was a yellow sticky note with Rodriguez's address curled up in the top right-hand corner. I stopped by on my way home.

A short young Mexican woman answered the door, her dark

hair held back by a bright yellow bandana, eyes shining black beneath it. A barefoot boy about two, in shorts and no shirt, clung to her skirt. A little dog was yapping above the sound of a baby crying in a room behind her, and a lusty Spanish-language soap opera was playing on a small wall-mounted television over her shoulder.

"Excuse me," I said. "Are you Mrs. Rodriguez?"

She shook her head. I wondered how much English she understood.

"My name is Mike McMahon," I said, slowly and too loudly. "Is this where Mrs. Rodriguez lives?"

"Not any more."

"She moved?"

"Yes, her husband drown in the reever, and she go back to Meheeco."

"Just like that?"

"Oh, si. She take the keeds and go back to leeve with her mother."

"When?"

"Thees morning. Driving. She get a ride from a man she know."

"Mrs. . . . *Senora?*"

"My name ees Juanita, and why do you want to know all thees?"

I paused for a moment. "I'm working with the sheriff's department. We're just trying to make sure that what happened to Mr. Rodriguez was, well, an accident."

"We all want to know that same thing," she said. "Everything was going so good for heem. And he not drink. Like most of them."

I thanked her for her time, gave her my card, and asked her to call me if she heard anything about Mr. Rodriguez or if Mrs. Rodriguez came back.

"Oh, she not coming back."

When I got home I called Becka at work.

"Who's this?" she said.

"Very funny."

"No, I'm serious. To whom am I speaking?"

"'*Whom*'? Oh that's right, you're an English professor."

"And who are you?"

"Becka, I—."

"Excuse me, Sir, but I have student papers to read, a paper of my own to work on, and a graduate student who wants to jump my bones."

I apologized for not having returned her phone call, and I apologized for having been out of touch for several days, and I apologized for being such a jerk, and I apologized for all of the American presidential assassinations, and then I told her about the tickets to the concert that night.

"Sir George Ivan Morrison. Van the Man."

"You're kidding," she said.

I had her.

"Nope. Stub Hub this afternoon.

"I don't know," she said. "*Lincoln*? "

Becka and I had a drink on the deck at Sam's in Tiburon before heading over to Berkeley, where we had a quick dinner before the concert. We got to the Community Theater plenty early, even though our fourth-row seats were reserved.

Van was in great form. Played stuff from almost every period, and even almost smiled once. Encore: Dylan's "It's All Over Now, Baby Blue," from which he went right into "My Funny Valentine" and "Send in the Clowns," then closed with an eight- or nine-minute "Gloria."

After the show we drove back over to Marin for a nightcap at the No Name Bar in Sausalito. I parked on the harbor side of the road, and we stood for a few minutes watching the sailboats slipped side by side in the cool fog, the air salty and wet. Inside, the No Name was dark and nearly empty. We sat in a back corner. Becka ordered a glass of chardonnay, and I had an Anchor Steam.

As good as the show had been, I was still preoccupied with the whole Johnny Sands case.

"You want to talk about it?"

"What?"

She shook her head and looked to the door. "If it's a case you're working on and you can't talk about it, I'll understand, but at least you can tell me that much."

I nodded and smiled. "Sorry, Babe," I said. "Yeah, it's a case, and there's not much to it really, it's just well, kinda close to home, that's all."

She reached across the table and took my hand, and I told her all I knew, from Sarah Rooney's stopping by my classroom to Pedro Rodriguez's death. She sipped her wine and listened.

"You think he was murdered?" she said.

"I kinda do, but it's going to be hard to prove. I mean cause of death was officially massive internal injuries caused by the car accident, which they say was caused by the cardiac arrest."

"So what're you going to do?"

"Find out why someone would want to kill Rooney, and then see if I can nail them?"

"Him," she said. "'Someone' is singular."

I scowled. "Him or her, then."

"I doubt it."

"Hey, women can be killers, too," I said.

"That's right. It's in their nature. Just look at history."

"Like Atilla the Honey?"

She tried not to, but laughed. I watched her thinking. "And Galigula?"

"Bitchard the Third?"

She looked around, then whispered. "Michael, that's *bad.*" She took a sip of her drink, then dabbed at her mouth with the corner of her napkin. "So essentially," she said, "you just need to find someone with a reason to kill him."

"Motive, Baby," I said. "We professionals say, 'motive.'"

— 8 —

The next morning, we slept in. Well, stayed in bed a long time anyway. The second best part was nailing the *New York Times* crossword puzzle together over coffee. Finally, Becka got up, showered, and dressed. I could hear the coffee maker in the kitchen. After she left, I got up, poured a cup of coffee, glanced at the Sporting Green—the Giants had beat the Dodgers, but I knew that—then went to the computer and did a quick Facebook search for Lester Corbin. I found one living in Santa Fe. I sent him a "friend" request and a message, told him I was working for Sarah Rooney, and gave him my phone number. He called the next day. I asked if I could visit.

He said to come on out and that he'd be happy to put me up for as long as I wanted—his bed and breakfast was called Hacienda de las Flores and was near the downtown plaza.

I bought a ticket for Albuquerque, reserved a rental car, and texted Raven asking her to feed Luther while I was gone. I called Becka from the airport.

"Santa Fe?" she said. "Jees! Can I go?"

"Look, I'll find us a nice place and make reservations for next fall. I kinda need to go alone this time. Besides, don't you have papers to read, or something?"

"Probably should . . . But, Santa Fe . . . "

"I'll call you when I get back," I said. "Just not . . . "

"Late for dinner?"

Used to be much funnier.

I had a two-hour layover in Phoenix. On a lark I Googled Connie Sands and found one in the White Pages that was probably her. The right age. Then I found a bar and watched a Suns-Pistons game and drank a couple of beers.

Phoenix. I think there are more polyester pants and white belts per capita in Phoenix than anywhere else in the world. And baseball caps with golf-ball makers' names on them. Thankfully, there's spring training—I've spent many afternoons over the years watching the Giants figure out their line-ups.

It was nearly six o'clock by the time I arrived in Albuquerque, got my car, and made my way out onto the freeway heading north. As I drove, my gaze was drawn to the Sandia Mountains, a stark and sudden range rising to over 10,000 feet, the northeastern outskirts of Albuquerque dwarfed by the range's towering south face—into which Johnny Sands' plane had slammed over forty-five years before.

I hadn't been to Albuquerque in several years, not since a summer in my early 20s when I'd followed an old girlfriend from Cal down. She was working on her Ph.D. in anthropology and spent her days at Anasazi Indian digs and her nights reading. I spent my days reading and fishing and my nights playing rhythm guitar in a little country band called the Rattlers. When we first had moved down, we thought we might stay, but she was so busy that after three months we hardly knew each other, and I had grown tired of the desert. I headed back to California about two months before she did and haven't seen her since.

I was amazed at Albuquerque's growth. The city had sprawled to the north and west, with rows upon rows of houses and subdivisions blanketing the plateau, which only a few years before had been home to the small retirement community of Rio Rancho. Now Rio Rancho was the fourth largest city in the state, thanks to the computer-chip industry and other companies that had taken advantage of the cheap land, making the area sort of a Silicon Valley of the southwest. And then there were the casinos, which were just starting to pop up the summer I spent in the area. Now most of the pueblos and reservations in the state had built sprawling casino-hotel-restaurant complexes, their electronic marquees advertising Jeep give-aways, loose slots, low-minimum blackjack tables, and the phone number for

Gamblers Anonymous.

If you want to, you can drive from Albuquerque to Santa Fe in an hour. It's about 60 miles. Anyone who knows Cruz's wouldn't want to, though. Cruz's is in Bernalillo, about fifteen miles north of Albuquerque, and has New Mexico's longest single-family-owned liquor license. 1932. Every square inch of the ceiling and every wall of the place is covered. Rusted bedpans. Moonshine bottles. Branding irons. Barbed wire. Old beer cans. Pistols. And hats. Cowboy hats, baseball hats, boaters, and fedoras, but mostly cowboy hats. All donated by the widows of former customers and many of them adorned with the birth and death dates of their owners. A John Deere baseball cap hanging from the ceiling read "Billy Sanchez 1924–1987."

I sat down at the bar and ordered a Bud draft from a young Hispanic waitress and nibbled from a bowl of peanuts.

"The old man still around?" I asked.

She smiled and shook her head. "Nope, died a year ago April. His grandson's running things now."

"Sorry to hear."

She shrugged. "He went the right way, that's for sure."

"The right way?"

"Worked up until the day he died. Walked in here about 10 o'clock one morning, served a customer a boilermaker, then set his keys, wallet, and gun on the bar, and walked into the men's room. We found him dead about an hour later. Another beer?"

I nodded and thought about Sal Cruz, working the bar every night the Rattlers played, serving up drinks and telling jokes and laughing. And always that bowl of green-chili stew that he had cooking and that he'd haul out when the bar shut down

He'd serve us each a big bowl, claiming that it was much better than coffee for sobering folks up.

I finished my beer, then went into the bathroom. Above the toilet was a framed photo of Sal, his craggy face grinning in the shadow of a huge-brimmed white cowboy hat. When I walked back out, the waitress was talking to some biker. I got into Santa Fe about 8:00 and headed straight for Tomasita's for a green-chile enchilada plate and a Margarita then pulled into the gravel parking lot of Hacienda de las Flores about 9:30, just as the moon came up over the Jemez Mountains

It had been a long day. The Corbins weren't in, but Sonja, the young woman who checked me in, showed me my room. She was tall and thin and wore a turquoise skirt and loose-fitting muslin blouse. A silver-and-turquiose Zuni sun-sign pendant hung from a thin silver necklace. She told me that the Corbins would be back at breakfast. I showered, lay down and read a Townes Van Zandt biography for about a half hour, and must have fallen asleep some time around 10:30.

I woke to the smell of strong French-roast coffee, cinnamon, and cornbread, and shaved, dressed, and walked down the hall to the dining room, where six small tables for four were scattered over the terra-cotta tile floor. Thankfully. One of the most irritating things I can think of is sitting around a big table at breakfast with eight strangers and being forced to introduce yourself and then talk to them while you eat. I grabbed a copy of the *The New Mexican* magazine from the desk in the hallway and sat down at a table overlooking an adobe-walled patio, shaded by old wisteria twining through the boards of a weathered pergola. Sonja appeared immediately and poured me a cup of coffee as a tall, nearly bald man walked out of the kitchen wiping his hands on his floury apron. Sonja introduced him as Lester Corbin.

"Nice to meet you, Mike," he said, sitting down. "Sleep okay?"

"Like a *bambino*," I said, handing him my card.

He smiled appreciatively.

Sonja set a coffee cup in front of him and filled it.

He took a thoughtful sip. "I was sorry to hear about Jim," he said. "How's Sarah holding up?" You could still hear the south in his voice all these years later.

"Okay. She'll be doing a whole hell of a lot better if we can find out how he died."

"You really think there's more to it?"

"I don't know. I just don't know yet why anyone would want to kill him."

He nodded and took another sip of his coffee. Sonja set a steaming plate of potatoes, green chiles, scrambled eggs, and two flour tortillas in front of me.

Corbin waited till she was headed back to the kitchen, then said, "Listen, when you first told me about it, I was pretty doubtful, but I've been thinking. Some things have happened around here. Weird things."

"How so?"

"We got broken into about a month ago. I didn't think much of it at the time, but I've got a studio, a music room, where I keep a lot of stuff. Guitars, two old Martins. Some recording gear. Vintage Fender bass. Someone broke in, turned everything inside out but didn't take a damn thing."

Sonja returned, topped my coffee. I nodded, rolled some

pototoes, eggs, and chiles into my tortilla, and watched Sonja walk back to the kitchen, her skirt swaying in the slanting sunlight. "Nothing?"

"Nothing."

"What do you think they were looking for?"

"I have no idea. Probably not my *carnitas* recipe."

"You said strange things. What else?"

"Well, just a couple days after that, Roger Sands called. Out of nowhere. Says that he's going to be recording and wants to cut some of our old songs."

"And . . . ?"

"I was the bass player, Mike. Johnny wrote those songs. I told Roger he was barking up the wrong tree. He seemed to get kinda pissed, then hung up."

I'd almost finished my improvised breakfast burrito and was starting to sweat a bit on my eyelids. A good sign. The coffee stayed hot in the thick clay mug, making it even better. I squeezed some honey onto my second tortilla, rolled it up, and took a huge bite. Sonja smiled at me from a nearby table she was clearing.

I swallowed, still watching Sonja as she disappeared down the hall, then nodded.

"This is bringing back a lot of weird stuff, man," Corbin said. "I mean, we've been here, Jees, almost twenty years now, and the crash was twenty-five years before that. All this Johnny Sands stuff seems like another lifetime." He held up his coffee cup for Sonja, and she came over and refilled it, then took my plate away.

"Even living this close to where the plane went down?"

He nodded. "You know, it used to be that when I'd drive by it, I'd think about that night, but then it just sort of slipped away. You move on." He laughed softly. "You better, after 45 years." He paused for a moment and looked out the window. "Except sometimes. When it's just like that clear summer night and I'm driving up from Albuquerque and I look over at the side of that mountain, and all of a sudden it's like the crash was yesterday. I'm always glad to get home. Christ, that was a horrible night."

"I'll bet." I wanted to get him talking about it, but I didn't want to make it any more painful than it was. "Where were you guys supposed to play next?"

"Amarillo. The next weekend. Jimmy and I were going to stick around Albuquerque and do a little sightseeing. Kevin was planning to fly back to North Carolina to see his girlfriend."

"Wait a minute. Kevin was planning to fly out that night?"

"Yeah, then he changed his mind. I don't know why."

"The same plane?"

"Uh huh. There weren't any flights out of Albuquerque that late so he'd chartered a little Cessna to take him up to Denver.

"But Johnny went instead? That didn't strike anybody as just a little bit strange?"

Sonja reappeared, held the coffee pot up, but I put my hand over my cup. She refilled Corbin's. He scooted back away from the table, crossed his ankles, and nodded. "I guess a little," he said. "But things were so hectic, chaotic, right after the crash that, well, I guess it just got lost in the shuffle."

A young couple, obviously recently showered, probably together, walked into the dining room, looked around, and chose a table as far from us as possible. They both wore khaki hiking shorts that looked like they'd just arrived L.L. Bean Express and handsome Teva sandals. He set his man bag on the table, pulled a chair out for her, then sat down and reached across it to take her little hand.

I could see Sonja rinsing dishes in the kitchen.

Corbin watched to make sure Sonja saw them walk in. "Only thing I wonder," he said, "is if it didn't have something to do with Kevin's breakdown. I mean, Jees, he's supposed to be on the plane, his brother goes instead, the plane goes down, I mean . . . " He trailed off.

"How long after the show till the plane took off?"

"About fifteen minutes. Silva always ran a pretty tight ship."

"He the one who arranged the flight?"

"I assume so. He usually did."

Corbin wiped his mouth with his napkin, grabbed his coffee cup, and said, "Let's go outside. You want a refill?"

"I'm good," I said, and followed him through some large French doors out onto the patio. Hollyhocks grew against one wall and a bird of paradise fanned out over some wrought-iron tables and rattan chairs.

"What was Silva like?" I asked as we sat down.

Corbin shook his head. "He was an odd bird, that guy. Didn't seem to have much of a life, except the band. Never got a much of read on him. Although I don't think we'd have ever made it without him."

"What all did he do for you guys?"

"Everything. Booked the gigs, arranged travel, recording contracts, set up studio time, handled all the press. Definitely got us out of Raleigh."

"What's he doing now?"

"Who knows? I never saw him after Johnny's funeral."

"You said you assume he booked the flight that night for Johnny?"

"Yeah, though I don't know. I do remember their fighting that night, though."

"Fighting?"

"Man, never seen anything like it. I mean, sometimes we'd get pissed at each other for some little thing, but then it'd blow over. Johnny and Kevin'd go at it sometimes, and then not even speak to each other for days. But once we got on stage everything fell right back into place."

"What were they fighting about?"

"I couldn't tell," Corbin said. "It was back stage right after the show, in Johnny's dressing room, and all three of them were yelling. I wouldn't have paid a whole lot of attention if it had just been Kevin and Johnny, but I could hear Silva right in there with them."

"But you don't remember what about?"

"I don't not remember, I just didn't hear. Last thing I heard was a door slam. A half hour later Johnny's plane's down."

"I know the boys' dad died when they were young," I said, "but the mom's still around, right? Living in Phoenix . . . ?"

Corbin smiled, shaking his head. "Yep. Still kickin'. Amazing. Lives in a little independent-care facility. Adobe Terraces. I visited a couple of times when we first moved to the southwest but I haven't seen her in, what, fifteen years. Still exchange Christmas cards, though."

"Jees," I said, "she must be . . . "

"Eighty-five, eighty-six . . . And doing great."

"Wow."

"Yeah, talk about some genes. If Johnny hadn't died he'd probably still be rockin'—and fending off the chicks."

— 9 —

I thanked Corbin for his time, went back to my room and opened up my laptop. I owed about 25 college kids an email.

Dear class,

Unfortunately, I'm stuck in New Mexico and won't be able to make it back to Marin in time for our class this evening, so I'm going to have to cancel. (I can hear your cheers from here . . .) For next week, please read Chapter 12 in Rockin' in the Free World *and watch the videos that I posted online. There will be a short quiz on the reading. Enjoy the videos. No change in presentation schedule. Final papers still due at our next-to-last meeting, May 5. I'll return them finals week. Remember, the assignment is to show how your artist fits into the traditions we've been talking about this semester.*

Mike

I hit Send, packed up, waved *adios* to Sonja on my way out, and drove back to Albuquerque and caught my flight. I had another layover in Phoenix, so I bumped my flight back another couple of hours and took an Uber out to Mrs. Sands' complex.

Adobe Terraces was an L-shaped single-story building surrounding a desert-landscaped courtyard area—prickly pear and tall grasses growing up out of mounded sand—and fronting a lush, rolling-hilled nine-hole golf course. The office and dining hall were at one end, a dozen or so golf carts parked at the other.

My driver let me out and I went in through the automatic doors of the main entrance. The dining area was on the far side of the room behind two totally out-of-place neo-classical columns. Two men and two women sat at one of the tables playing cards. A young woman sat at the front desk looking at a computer screen. Her name tag said "Carmen." I introduced myself and asked about Mrs. Sands.

"Oh, Connie," she said. "Everyone knows Connie."

I asked if I could see her.

"I don't know why not. Let me give her a call."

A few minutes later a tall woman with a little Bichon Frise on a leash was walking down the hall toward me. She wore a navy skirt and white blouse, her gray hair short and neat, falling in bangs across her forehead. She looked young for mid-eighties. Probably the desert air and sunshine. In addition to those genes.

She picked up the dog with one hand and held the other out to shake. "Connie Sands," she said. "This is Ella." Ella had a green ribbon tied into the fur on the side of her head. She yapped.

Mrs. Sands rolled her eyes. "I named her before I heard her sing." You could still hear North Carolina in her voice, as well.

We sat down in a couple of large leather chairs in a little room off the dining area, and Mrs. Sands set Ella down on the carpet. Ella came over and sniffed my boots and yapped again.

"Ella," Mrs. Sands said.

"It's okay," I said. "Probably smells my Luther."

"Luther?"

"My Newfoundland."

Mrs. Sands shuddered. "Don't they look like bears?"

"Friendlier," I said. "If they like you."

Carmen came over. "Can I get you some coffee or something? Juice?"

"Coffee sounds delicious, Carmen," Mrs. Sands said.

"Two," I said. Ella tried to jump up onto my lap. I gave her a little shove with my boot. She rolled onto the carpet, regained her footing, and scooted across the floor and glared at me from underneath a Georgia O'Keeffe print.

Carmen returned a minute or so later with a silver tray with two porcelain cups, a silver creamer, and a tall, elegant silver urn set on a paper-lace doily. She set the tray down on the coffee table, and poured two cups. We each took one.

"I'm really sorry to bother you, Mrs. Sands," I said, "but I'm doing some research on the Johnny Sands Band and—"

She cut me off. "No bother," she said, sipping her coffee. "Ask anybody. It's about all I talk about anyway." She set her coffee down on a napkin on the table. "I was sorry to hear about Jim Rooney. I hardly knew him, but I know he meant a lot to the boys. Kevin even still talks about him sometimes."

"Does Kevin know, or I guess remember, how Johnny died?" I asked.

"Oh, he remembers. He remembers a lot more than people give him credit for. At least off and on. Of course, I don't get up there much any more, but sometimes when I'd visit him he wouldn't even recognize me, and other times we'd sit and talk and he'd remember the tiniest of details."

"Not even recognize you? Must have been hard."

"Oh, yeah." She stood up. "Come with me." She led me through the dining room to a hallway, then stopped in front of a door with a smiling photo of her above the number 117, slowly turned the knob and pushed it open. I followed her inside. The walls were covered with framed gold records, posters of the band, framed lyrics scribbled on scratch paper, and photographs of Johnny and Kevin as young boys. A gorgeous maple Baldwin spinet piano was up against one wall, and a blond Fender Telecaster stood in a guitar stand in the corner. Another wall was lined corner to corner and floor to ceiling with books. She walked over to the bookshelf. I followed.

"This is how Johnny escaped," she said. She pulled out a book of poetry by Walt Whitman, thumbed through it. I looked more closely. The books were almost all poetry. English romantics, Blake, Wordsworth, Keats. And Americans, Whitman, Frost, Sandburg, cummings, Jeffers. Ginsberg.

"Escaped?"

"My husband." She pushed the book back onto the shelf. "Their father died when they were very young, and I remarried. A wonderful man in a lot of ways. But he drank a lot, and when he drank he wasn't a wonderful man. And the boys took the worst of it. He just never could accept them as his own, but . . . "

I nodded.

"Kevin didn't have an escape. Except his music. And even then people were always praising Johnny, and I think that was painful for Kevin."

I pulled out a copy of Whitman's *Leaves of Grass*, turned it over to the familiar gray-haired-and-bearded photo on the back cover, then put it back on the shelf and walked over to the wall of framed lyrics. Though most were fragments and early versions of Johnny Sands Band songs, one was printed up in an ornate, almost Old Englishy font on powder-blue paper.

"'Danny Boy'?" I said.

Mrs. Sands smiled, nodded, and took a wistful breath. "Johnny's very favorite song," she said. "I used to sing it to the boys when they were babies. He hated it for a while, or said he did. But then when he was about fifteen and just getting serious about his own music, he was almost obsessed with it. In fact, he even wanted to record it. He and Kevin argued about that for years."

"Argued?"

"Kevin didn't love the song like Johnny did."

"I get that."

"But Johnny loved to read. Maybe even more than play music, even though the music came so naturally to him. He never made very good grades in school, but give him a book, the longer the better, and we wouldn't see him till he was done with it."

"What happened to . . . ?"

"My husband?"

"Yeah."

"I finally got smart. He came home one night and got a little, well, physical. I walked out. He never contested the divorce, and I haven't seen him since."

"Larry Grant?"

"Larry Grant."

I stepped away from the wall.

She shrugged. "Funny, huh? Anyway, I had that 'Danny Boy' framed for Johnny. It's the one thing I really wish he could come back and see."

She turned and walked to a sofa, on which Ella had taken up residence. Mrs. Sands picked her up. "Sit down?"

"I'd like to," I said, "but I really ought to be going. I can't thank you enough for your time."

"Already?" she said. "I thought maybe I'd be able to talk you into dinner. The food's actually not bad here."

I looked at my watch. "Gee, thanks, but I've got a plane to catch. I've got to be getting back."

She dropped Ella gently onto the floor.

I tried to think of a way to ask delicately, but couldn't. "Mrs. Sands? From what I understand, Kevin was supposed to be on that plane, but then at the last minute . . . "

"I know," she said. "I've wondered about that all these years."

"So you don't have any idea why Johnny might have taken his place?"

"Only that he was coming out to see me. He'd called earlier that afternoon and said he wanted to see me, to talk about something."

"And you have no idea what that was?"

"Oh, I don't know . . . " She shook her head. "Maybe, but none of that matters now."

"Maybe it does," I said.

She shook her head again. "It's been hard," she said, "and it was really hard at first. Please."

"Sorry," I said, "but I have one last question."

"Sure."

"Those songs Johnny wrote, they were amazing. They still are. They get covered all the time . . . "

She nodded.

"They must be making a fortune in royalties. Who . . . where . . . ?"

"Where's the money going?"

"Exactly."

She shrugged. "I know, I've always thought there should be more out there."

"But you've never looked into it, or hired someone to?"

She shook her head. "I get enough to get by on, and it's how we pay for Kevin's care. But . . . " She trailed off.

I smiled, nodded, and looked down at Ella, who didn't seem quite so annoying all of a sudden. I reached down and patted her little head. "I like her ribbon."

"She likes you," Mrs. Sands said.

I took an Uber back to the airport, bumped my flight back again, to the next morning, and took a shuttle to a generic airport hotel. I checked in, dropped my bags in my room, texted Raven about feeding Luther, and went for a swim. It seemed odd to be swimming indoors in the middle of the sunbelt, but it felt good anyway, and after a thousand yards I felt I'd earned myself a beer.

I watched a bit of news on CNN, thought about going out to watch the D-Backs but instead took an Uber out to a bar downtown, the Cactus Club, a loud little place with pool tables in the back and cowboys in Wranglers bent over their cues, glasses and half-empty pitchers of beer on every table. Surprisingly full for a Monday night. I sat at the bar with a pitcher of my own, thought about setting a quarter on a pool-table rail and waiting for a game but listened to the house band instead. The Redrocks were pretty decent—playing mostly covers of Brad Paisley and Kenny Chesney, with an occasional Merle Haggard or George Jones tune. The vocalist, who also played fiddle, and the keyboard player both had some downright likable honky-tonk chops.

I was just about to head down the street when they announced a break and stepped off the stage. A young woman in cowboy boots, a long gingham skirt, and soft orange hair tumbling halfway down her back walked out onto the stage. She smiled awkwardly, tuned up her Gibson Hummingbird, and then without a word launched into the prettiest version of "Wildwood Flower" I'd ever heard. I poured the last of my pitcher into my mug and listened while she sang songs about rodeoin', bein' done wrong, and finding Jesus and salvation on the other side. Imagine a cross between Mother Maybell Carter and Rita Hayworth. By her third song, the pool tables in the back had all grown quiet, and the cowboys all stood rapt, some actually holding hands with their wives.

She finished up with Gram Parsons' "Return of the Grievous Angel" and nodded toward someone offstage. Then she smiled and in a sweet southern drawl introduced Bobby, a skinny, pony-tailed kid who looked 17 and had joined her on stage holding a fiddle to his chin. He nodded and drew the bow across a string. "And my name's Ginger," she said. "We're just gonna do a few more for you." A collective groan rose from back by the pool tables. She smiled again. "Thank you."

She looked to Bobby, who nodded and counted out the beat with the pointy toe of a black boot, and then played the chorus to "Goodnight, Irene," before Ginger started in. "Sometimes I live in the country . . . " On the last verse, the fiddle player picked up the pace for a moment, then slowed it way down, and set his fiddle on the floor beside him. Then he tucked his thumb into his belt and they did a duet on "Canaan's Land" that blew the crowd away. Then they did one that blew *me* away: "Out on a Limb," from the second Johnny Sands album. Slowed way down, with harmonies that soared above the beer-soaked room. On the last verse, Ginger let her guitar hang by its strap, cupped her hand behind her ear and closed her eyes, and they sang.

"All alone in a tree and out on a limb
Singing my song, hellbound by hymns."

They bowed, then stepped off the stage, the cowboys whistling and hollering for all they were worth. I watched her walk over to the bar, take the bottle of beer the bartender handed her, then swivel down onto a stool to watch the Redrocks take the stage. Her fiddle player had disappeared.

I grabbed my mug and walked over to her. She looked up and smiled.

"Beautiful," I said.

"Thank you."

"I really like how you did that Johnny Sands tune."

She smiled again. "Thanks. We've been workin' on it. That was the first time we played it in public."

"Your arrangement?"

She shook her head and took a pull on her beer. "Bobby's. His idea, too. I never thought it would work."

I nodded to the bartender, and ordered two more beers. "It does, though." I set a ten-dollar bill on the bar. "He wrote some great songs didn't he?"

"You play?"

I shrugged. "Used to."

"Used to? Why used to?"

The bartender set the beers in front of us and slid the bill off the table.

"Thanks," she said.

"Sure . . . Oh, I don't know. Too old?" I was hoping for a laugh and a "No way" but got a shrug instead.

Suddenly her face brightened as she caught sight of someone coming in the front door. "Over here," she mouthed, waving the very beer that I had bought for her as a tall bearded man in dark glasses and a gray blazer over a black t-shirt nodded and walked toward us. She stood as he approached. "How'd it go?" he said. Ginger shrugged.

He put his arm around her. "Sorry I couldn't make it, Babe," he said as she stood up, smiled at me, and said, "Thanks for the beer." They walked over to the side of the stage, where he picked up her guitar case and led her out the door.

The Redrocks were rocking now—the Stones' "Sweet Virginia"— and the place was getting loud with shouting and clacking pool balls. I drank the last of my beer and headed out to the street. It was still warm, and I took a deep breath of the dry desert air. It would have been nice about then if Becka were with me. I walked back to my room, took my boots off, and fell asleep with my jeans and t-shirt on. When I woke up I smelled and looked like hell.

— 10 —

I flew into SFO late Tuesday afternoon, drove across the Golden Gate Bridge as the sun was falling toward the Pacific horizon, and got home just before six. I dropped my overnight bag inside the door, where Luther sniffed it disapprovingly. I grabbed a cold slice of pepperoni pizza out of the refrigerator and munched on it while I fed him and watched him eat. Then I went straight down the hallway to the bedroom, where I lay back on my bed.

But immediately, something didn't feel right. I sat up and looked around. The top drawer of my dresser was open, and a pair of boxer shorts hung out loosely. I went over and looked inside. Empty. Goddammit.

Break-in! Again.

"Luther!"

Luther came bounding in, but saw I was angry, and turned to go back down the hall.

"Luther, come back here."

He came up to me, nuzzled my knee, then hung his head. I couldn't stay angry. After all, he'd been left alone for two days. He'd been bored.

"Sorry, dude. You know I hate leaving you like that."

He looked up and wagged his tail.

I found six pairs of socks in the living room—one under the coffee table, one nudged into a corner behind a floor lamp—but decided to wait until morning to look for the rest. I knew that at least a couple of pairs wouldn't turn up at all.

I sort of wished I'd never installed that extra-large doggie door to let him get in out of the rain.

I got up, went into the kitchen, grabbed a couple of treats out of his Tupperware bowl, and fed him from my open hand. "Good night, Irene," I said. "See you in the A.M."

I woke at nine, showered, and drank some coffee and ate a toasted bagel while I read the *Chronicle.* At ten, I phoned Becka.

"Just get in?"

"Last night."

"Oh."

"'Oh'?"

"Oh."

"I missed you," I said.

"How was Santa Fe?"

"Okay. You want to come over tonight?"

"I don't think so."

"Papers to read?"

"No."

"What's wrong?"

"Oh, I'm just tired of it all," she said.

Oh, Jees. Here it comes. "What?"

"Oh, Michael, you know. We've talked about it. We just need to decide where we're going, even *if* we're going. Everything just seems so, well, ill-defined."

"'Ill-defined'?" What's she want, a Funk and Wagnell's? Man likes woman. Woman likes man. They spend time together.

But not all of it.

"Yeah, you know. I'm not even sure what we have anymore."

I took a deep breath.

She must have heard it. "Maybe you don't need to know, but I just feel like, well, I'm almost 40, and I'm tired, that's all. Of waiting. Not knowing. Guessing."

"Look, Babe, I had to go out of town, on business. That's my work. I don't know what—"

"That's just it, you don't know. And that's fine. But I, well, I'll see you, okay. I'll talk to you. But not right now."

"Okay," I said. "Talk to you."

"Bye, Michael."

"Bye, Babe."

And she hung up.

Shit. Nothing was working. I wasn't playing any music. My love life was in shambles, and I'd spent an awful lot of Sarah Rooney's money to learn not much at all about who, if anyone, killed her husband. Luther watched me through the sliding-glass door, wanting big-time to go for a walk. I did him one better— took him for a long hike on Mt. Tam. I listened to Johnny Sands through my Bose earbuds.

For some reason one song haunted me. "Out on a Limb." I couldn't get it out of my head.

When I got home, I checked my email. I wanted to make sure none of my students had questions about the cancelled class. Sure enough, there was a note in my inbox from Chet Porter, a smart, quiet kid planning to transfer to Cal and major in English. He was tall and thin and wore plaid flannel shirts,

Malcolm X glasses and a fuzzy dark brew-pub beard.

Hey Mike, Hope u had a good time in New Mexico we missed you, I'm totally caught up on the homework and watched those videos u assigned, I was wondering, I know, u don't have office hours but would it be possible to meet on campus sometime this week?
Chet Porter

He was right about that—I didn't have office hours. Or even an office to hold them in. It was one of the good-news-bad-news things about being a part-timer. The full-time instructors were required to keep five hours a week. They also had their own private offices. Part-timers shared a common faculty room with a handful of desks and computers where they were encouraged to meet students. Sometimes we met them in our cars in the parking lot.

I fought the urge to tell him that using "u" for "you" in notes to instructors wasn't a very good way to curry favor with them. Also that he'd have to learn, how to use, commas if he wanted to, be, an, English major.

Thanks for the note, Chet. Sure, I'd be happy to meet you. Kent 105 is usually available. When's a good time?
Mike
Thank u, the sooner the better, what works for u?

We set up a meeting for 10:00 AM Friday.

I went into the living room and put on *Time of Sands*. I stared at the CD cover, Johnny with his distant, hiding-from-the-world look, the others looking like hillbilly moonshiners. I looked closely at Kevin. I'd need to talk to him, if he were up for it.

I also needed to get down to Los Angeles to talk to Roger. I phoned Sarah Rooney for his phone number, and called him and told him that I was working on the Jim Rooney case and was going to be in the area. He agreed to meet with me the next day. I booked a 9:30 United flight out of San Francisco, reserved a car, and tried to call Becka. She didn't answer. I missed the hell out of her.

I went into the office and did some internet research on schizophrenia.

I wasn't surprised how much was written on the disease, especially as the more I read the more I realized how little was actually known. In fact, a lot of it was just clinical jargon for what I already knew. A mental disorder ranging from mild to severe, typically with hallucinations, disordered thinking, withdrawal from reality. Four main types: simple, hebephrenic, catatonic, and paranoid. I was mainly interested in two things. One, how bad off Kevin was, and two, how his might have been triggered. Obviously, I wasn't going to learn anything about Kevin from reading about the disease in general, and there didn't seem to be too much evidence about how it's triggered. Trauma, stress, genetics—they all seemed to play a part. I wondered if Johnny's death had anything to with it.

After an hour or so, I logged off and went to bed.

— 11 —

I got into LAX a little after 11:00 and fell for the clerk's suggestion to upgrade my rental car. But the cool black Camaro convertible was perfect. I paired my phone, hit the iTunes icon, scrolled to my Beach Boys playlist and went looking for some lunch.

Something about driving around Los Angeles in the springtime, before the air gets heavy and the smog hangs in the valley and hides the mountains. Usually it cheers me right up. But even with the top down I just felt like some chump trying to act like he had his shit together. On top of that, I had trouble finding a place to eat. Mostly fast-food and new-age southern California food. Tofu-and-hummus pizza didn't sound very appetizing, and I didn't really feel like sitting at a picnic table under a canvas awning at a Serbian-Korean taco truck, no matter how good I knew the food would be. Finally, I found a little hole-in-the-wall where I sat at the bar and ate a drippy burger with bacon and cheddar cheese that I washed down with a pint of some local IPA. Afterward, I felt like taking a nap, but I'd told Roger I'd be at his apartment by 2:00. I pulled into the parking lot at about five of.

Roger Sands lived in 146B of the Casas del Sol, a townhouse complex that sprawled over several acres, each tan stucco unit looking exactly like the next, the grounds meticulously maintained, mounds of deep green grass, beds of agapanthus and redwood bark, and young plum and crape myrtle trees. Number

146B was on the inside of a cluster of buildings that surrounded a large pool, where a couple of women were sunbathing, lying on their stomachs on lounge chairs. It looked like their bikini tops might be unhooked, so I wandered over to check. They were. Sheryl Crow sang from hidden speakers—probably disguised as landscaping rocks. I turned, walked over to 146 and climbed the stairs to B, and knocked on Roger Sands' door.

Roger Sands looked like he had just gotten out of bed. He wore a pair of black jeans, white socks, and a Golds Gym t-shirt, revealing a tattoo of a curling wave on his upper left arm and some kind of tribal scrawl on his lower right, a musical quarter note inked onto his neck under his left ear. His dark hair was short and rumpled, and he needed to shave. But then that would have made him look less like a movie star.

"Come on in," he said after I'd handed him my card and introduced myself. "Sorry." He turned up his hands, then led me into the cluttered front room. A sunburst Fender Stratocaster lay across the arms of a large easy chair, its cord snaking across the room to a little Fender Champ practice amp in the corner. The coffee table was covered with celebrity magazines, sheet music, and the swimsuit issue of *Sports Illustrated*. The *L.A. Times* sports section was opened up on the floor, the lead story about a Dodgers loss. Finally some good news.

Roger picked up a cup of coffee off the counter, and walked around the faux-tile bar into the kitchen. "Coffee?"

"Sure," I said.

He took a cup from the sink, rinsed it out, touched two fingers to the side of a Mr. Coffee coffee maker, then poured a cup. "Want anything in it?"

I shook my head.

"Good. I don't think I have anything."

He handed me the coffee cup over the bar, then walked back around into the living room. He moved his guitar, indicating for me to sit down, then sat down on the couch. "Sorry," he said again. "Up late last night"

I nodded. "Playing music?"

"Yeah, but not last night. Some friends were playing out at the Canyon Club. You know it?"

I did.

"Didn't get in till about four."

"Got it," I said.

Roger took a sip of his coffee and looked at me over the top of the cup. Then he looked at my card. "So," he said. "Mr. Mc-Mahon. Private investigator. Mill Valley, California. What can I do you for?"

"I told you last night," I said. "I'm working on the Jim Rooney case."

He set my card down and took another swallow of coffee. "Bummer, wasn't it?"

"Sure was."

"I doubt I can help."

"Apparently Jim Rooney was writing a book about the Johnny Sands Band, in fact had just finished it, when he died. His wife thinks there might have been something in it that someone didn't want people to read about." I watched him closely to see how much he might know.

"Really? I'd like to read a book like that. Might learn something." If he knew about the book, he didn't show it.

"At any rate, I was hoping maybe you could tell me a little bit about how you fit into the whole band thing, what it's been like being the son of Johnny Sands, what—"

"Mr. McMahon, I wasn't even one when my dad died." He stood, coffee cup in hand, and went to the window, looked down onto the pool, probably at those soft bare backs. "When I was growing up Mom never even talked about the band, or my dad. She used to take me up to see my uncle Kevin in the nut house when I was a kid, but that's it." He turned to look at me, started to talk, stopped, then started again. "I didn't even know who Johnny Sands was until I was about 12. And then when she did tell me, all I knew was that he'd left her enough money for both of us to get by on." He walked back over and set his cup down on the coffee table.

I nodded, looking around, wondering whether I ought to ask, then did. "Just 'get by'?"

"I know, I know. That estate should be worth a fortune. The fucking royalties. But what the hell? Where the fuck did it go?" He reached for a pack of cigarettes on the coffee table, lit one, waved out the match, and took a long drag. "More coffee?"

I shook my head.

"It's why I live in this shithole." He smiled again. "Some day, though . . . "

"So you play music?"

"Play some music, yeah. I'm also in the Screen Extras Guild. Crowd scenes, usually. A hundred-seventy bucks a day for standing around eating studio food and waiting for someone to say 'jump.' Remember the crowd scene in *Running from Danger*?"

He took another pull on his cigarette and didn't see me shake my head or hear me say, "Missed that one."

"Remember everyone comes rushing out onto the steps of the courthouse right after the guilty verdict? That's me just over De Niro's left shoulder."

I nodded. "Must be interesting."

"What I'd really like is to get a speaking part. They fuck with you, though. You can't get a speaking part unless you're in the Screen Actors Guild, but you can't join the Screen Actors Guild until you've had a speaking part."

"When was the last time you were up in the Bay Area?"

He looked at me sharply, almost as though he'd forgotten I was there and had been just rambling on to himself.

"Frisco?"

"San Francisco. "

He took a breath and seemed to be doing some mental math. Very basic mental math. "About six months. Since last July."

"That's nine months."

"Whatever . . . I went up to see an old girlfriend. She was housesitting an apartment in Frisco, out by the beach."

"San Francisco?"

"Whatever."

"And you haven't been back since?"

He shrugged. "Can't say that I have."

"Why did you call Sarah Rooney a couple of weeks ago?"

He looked up, startled, took a drag on his cigarette, and tried to look non-plussed. Then he shrugged again. "Business, man. I'm thinking of recording, and I just want to make sure, you know, it's cool with the lawyers. And the band's family."

"I see, and Lester Corbin?"

He smiled. "You do your homework, don't you?"

"Business, man."

"Same thing. Just trying to make sure that when I go into the studios I'm not doing anything that ain't kosher."

"Did you know the Rooneys?"

He snubbed his cigarette out in a pizza crust on a paper plate on the coffee table. "I told you, I never knew any of them. I think Mom wanted it that way."

"But you knew Lester Corbin."

"Not even. That was the first time I ever talked to him. Honestly, I never knew anyone in the Johnny Sands Band except ol' Uncle Kev. Not my dad, obviously. Not Corbin. Not Jim Rooney."

"All right," I said. "Just asking. It's my job." I decided to try one more. "What about your grandmother?"

He looked up, caught off guard. "My dad's mom?"

"Your dad's mom."

"What about her?"

"Ever meet her?"

"No." He lit another cigarette.

"When's the last time you saw your mom?"

He licked his thumb and forefinger and pinched out the flame on the match, tossed it on the paper plate, and stood up. "Four or five years."

I understood that the margin of error meant that that could mean between two and eight.

"I moved out when I was 23, seen her a couple of times since. She used to call from time to time, but we haven't even talked in a couple of years." He looked at his watch.

"You know where she is?"

"Last I heard, Palm Springs."

"What about your other grandparents, on your mom's side?"

"Mom and I lived with them when I was little," he said. "They passed when I was high school." He stood up, went into the bathroom, and kept talking with the door open, a bit more loudly over the splashing. "Listen, I got an appointment at 3."

It was 2:45.

"I hate to run you out of here," he said, "but I'm meeting someone about an idea for a screenplay we're working on."

I flipped through the magazines on the coffee table. "Can I give you a ride?"

I heard the toilet flush, and Roger walked out zipping up his fly. "Thanks," he said. "But I need my car." He went into the kitchen and took a Dodgers cap off the back of a chair and pulled it over his head, backward. "I hope I was helpful. I'm sure Sarah'd like to know who killed Jim, if someone did." He grabbed some keys and a wallet off the kitchen counter and went to the door, opened it, and turned to me.

I stood, and he followed me outside, pulling the door closed behind him. "If you think of anything else," I said. "Anything your mom might have said about the old days with the band, let me know, okay?"

"Sure, man. Got your card."

We shook hands then, and he went over to his car, a newer black BMW 3 series with an open sunroof. I went back to my rental Camaro, watched him pull out of the parking lot, and then followed him down the street. As soon as we were into traffic, he began a series of zigzag turns, finally circling right back to the parking lot of the Casas del Sol, where he pulled into his space, got out, and trotted back up to 146B, his shitty blue Dodgers cap in his hand.

— 12 —

I thought about sticking around, but an afternoon in Los Angeles was about all I could take. Besides, I was sure that Roger had just used his little ruse to get rid of me, not to clear the way for some dastardly crime he was about to commit. On top of that, I was pretty convinced I had learned all from him that I was going to. At least for now.

I'd also told Chet Porter that I'd meet him the next day.

I drove back to the airport, dropped off the car, and caught a 4:30 flight to SFO. By 8:00, I was at the bar at the Marin Brewing Company on my second pint of San Quentin Break-Out Stout. The Giants were pummeling the Rockies on the big-screen TV, and I was finishing up a basket of fish and chips.

I got home just after nine, took Luther out for a short walk, went to bed, and slept without stirring until 7:30. I fixed some coffee, read the *Chronicle*, and went through yesterday's mail. Mostly bulk-mailed crap, except for my *Rolling Stone*. Then I checked my email and found a note from Lester Corbin.

Hi Mike,

I enjoyed meeting with you, I hope I was at least a little bit helpful, I thought of something else yesterday, although you've probably already looked into it. There was a guy named Ted Knowlton that used to hang around with the band. Especially him and Johnny, sort of a roadie, and whenever we'd get to a new town, the two of them would take off. Ted was back stage at the show the night Johnny died, the only time I saw him after that was at the funeral. He was by himself in the back and didn't come over to Johnny's mom's house afterward. Probably doesn't mean much, but you did say anything at all might be helpful. I hope your trip back to California was good. Give my regards to Sarah and remember you're always welcome here at the inn.

Best,
LC

Ted Knowlton. No, I hadn't already looked into it. I'd never heard of Ted Knowlton. Of all the people I'd talked to, Corbin was the first to mention him at all. I called Sarah Rooney and we made a date for lunch the next day at Louie Chan's in Mill Valley. Then I headed over to College of Marin to meet Chet Porter.

He was sitting against the wall in the hallway outside Kent 105 when I got there. He stood, followed me inside, and we sat across from each other at the end of a long table in the middle of the room. A couple of other part-time instructors were working on computers at desks in cubicles along the far wall.

Porter set his messenger bag on the table in front of him and pulled out *Sandy Morning*.

"You like their stuff?" I asked.

"Yeah, I really do. I thought I was all about electronic music and techno, but this stuff, somehow it just gets to me. I mean, my generation's music just doesn't have, well, *soul*.

I couldn't have agreed more.

"I know I proposed my final paper about Kraftwerk . . ."

"I'm actually looking forward to it," I said. "I don't know much about them, and you seem like you're up to the job."

"Thanks. But if it's not too late, I'd like to change my paper topic."

Ordinarily, a student's changing paper topics sends up all kinds of red flags. Students put the work off, panic, and then buy one online, or have their girlfriend write it for them. But I had faith in this kid.

He held up *Sandy Morning* again, giving me a questioning look.

"Really?" I said. "The Johnny Sands band?"

He nodded. "Actually, Johnny Sands himself."

I mulled it over for a minute. "I really like the idea," I said, "and I'd much rather read about Johnny Sands than Kraftwerk anyway."

"Awesome," he said.

"One thing."

"What's that?"

"You're a smart guy, hard worker. So I'm trusting that you won't dwell on the obvious . . . "

"Obvious?"

"Well, the whole plane-crash thing. Might be worth mentioning in passing, but I don't want a paper that's a list of rock stars who've died in plane crashes."

He scowled. Clearly not his plan. "Of course," he said.

"Good."

He paused, took a small breath, looked away for moment, then back at me. "The thing is, I feel like Johnny Sands might have been gay."

He'd caught me off guard. "Uh . . . I don't think so. What makes you think . . . ?"

Porter was tentative. He shrugged, fumbled with the strap on his messenger bag. "I don't know, I mean, well, I kinda feel like he was trying to come out in some of those songs." He looked away. I nodded thoughtfully, trying not to let on that I thought he was way off base.

"Such as?"

"Well the one that I can't get out of my head is 'Out on a Limb.'"

"Oh, come on, I don't even think they used the word 'out' like that back then."

Porter winced. "I think they did. I mean, you're the teacher, but I think they did. In fact, like, I know they did." He smiled. "Google is my friend."

"Look, Johnny Sands had a kid, and . . . a girfriend."

"I know."

I realized that that wasn't much of an argument.

"He wrote some great songs, didn't he?" Porter said.

"Some of the greatest."

We talked music small talk for a few more minutes. He seemed as aware as I was that our exchange had been a bit awkward. It was too late to walk back my comment about Johnny's having a kid and girlfriend. The conversation was running out of steam.

"Listen," I said. "I don't know exactly where you're going with your theory, but go for it. I've been encouraging you guys to take chances in your writing."

"To go out on a limb?"

"To go out on a limb."

"Thanks," he said, slipping *Sandy Morning* back into his messenger bag. "And thanks for taking the time to come down and meet with me."

"Of course," I said.

He stood. "See you Monday night. Have a good weekend."

"You too," I said, and watched him walk through the door and out into the hallway.

Sarah was already seated when I got to Louis Chan's, sipping from a glass of iced tea and nibbling from a plate of wontons. She wore a low-cut blouse that showed a hint of her upper breasts, tanned and lightly mottled and complemented by a narrow gold chain. Her hair was brushed down over her shoulders, held away from her forehead by a white elastic headband.

I sat down across from her and reached for a wonton.

"Drink?" she said.

"Sure." I looked around for a waitress, who was heading toward the table with a glass of water on a tray. I ordered a Lagunitas IPA and opened the menu.

"The special looks good," Sarah said.

"For two?"

"Sure."

The waitress reappeared with my beer, and we ordered. Cashew chicken, stir-fried broccoli, lo fun noodles, and fried rice with shrimp. "So," she said, "how's it going?"

I took a sip of beer, wiped the foam off my upper lip with my napkin, and shrugged. "I'm not sure."

"Meaning?"

"Meaning I've got more questions than I had before, but I've also found out some interesting things." I told her about meeting with Lester Corbin, Mrs. Sands, and Roger. She listened, sipping her drink.

The waitress brought our lunch, setting the steaming plates on the table in front of us. It looked like enough for a party of twelve. "Can I get you anything else?"

"I don't think so," I said.

Sarah spooned a small portion of everything onto each of our plates. I dished up more appropriate amounts onto mine.

I took my chopsticks in hand and pinched a big bite of noodles. Excellent, as usual.

Sarah tried the cashew chicken first, nodding approvingly. "Roger Sands is a liar," she said, picking up a piece of stir-fried broccoli and not looking up.

I set my chopsticks down. "A liar?"

"A liar."

"How so?"

She shook her head and punched her chopsticks into her pile of noodles. "Let me count the ways."

I took a bite and waited for her continue.

"First of all," she said. "Roger *does* know, or at least has met, some of those people he claims he hasn't. I know for a fact, that he met my husband. Roger might have been young, but it was after Jim and I were married, so he'd remember. Also, he didn't just move out of his mom's house when he was 23. She booted him out."

I nodded and told her about how my meeting with Roger had ended, Roger's bogus reason for leaving, then circling back to his place. I didn't mention the Dodgers cap.

"So where does that leave us?" she said, pushing her plate aside.

I took a breath. "I'm not sure. I mean, he seems like kind of a snake, but I'm not sure he'd . . . "

"Kill Jimmy?"

"Or have a reason to," I said, dishing up some more vegetables and chicken.

"What about royalties?" she said.

"I don't know. He says what everyone else says, that there's not as much as maybe there should be . . . "

The waitress brought a plate with two fortune cookies and the folder with the bill, and a busboy cleared our table. "One more thing," I said. "What do you know about Ted Knowlton?"

"Ted Knowlton? Who's he?"

I told her about Lester Corbin's email as we cracked open our fortune cookies. She took out hers, read it, and smiled. "Wrong," she said. "'Your love life will soon take a turn for the better.'"

I laughed. "That should've been mine. "Even wronger."

"What's yours say?"

I read it and smiled. "Now that's a fortune. 'Trust a man's eyes, not his words.'"

She smiled.

"Sexist?" I asked.

"Not at all. Just true. You can trust a woman's words."

I nodded, and she folded up her napkin, dropped it on the

table, and stood up. "Ted Knowlton?" she said again, as though trying to place him in the picture. "I don't think so."

We walked toward the door.

"According to Corbin, he was some kind of roadie."

"I'm sure Jimmy never said anything about him."

"Well, if you remember anything," I said, "give me a call."

"Of course," she said, walking toward a gorgeous forest green 1960 Mercedes 220 in the parking lot.

— 13 —

When I got home, there was a note on my kitchen table, with my house key on top of it. Becka had been by to pick up "some things," she'd written, and figured she didn't need the key any more. I went into the bathroom. Her robe, lotion, and toothbrush were gone, but there was a single yellow rose in a tall, slim glass vase beside the sink.

I called her even though I knew she was in class and left a message thanking her for the rose. Then I phoned Mrs. Sands in Phoenix.

I got right to the point: Did she know Ted Knowlton?

There was a long pause. Then she said, "Sure, Teddy Knowlton. I think there were three Knowlton boys. Teddy, Billy, and Paul. Why?"

I told her about Lester Corbin's email.

"Ted Knowlton?" she said again. "I think he was in the class between Johnny's and Kevin's. I don't think they buddied around all that much. He was working for the band?"

"I guess so, and apparently he and Johnny got to be pretty good friends."

"Well, I don't know what the connection might be . . . "

"Whatever happened to the family?" I asked.

"I don't know, Mike. I pretty much lost track of everybody once I left Raleigh. I guess the family might still be around. His parents' names were, what were they? Everett, I think. Everett and Lucy. Of course, they'd be about my age."

I thanked her for her time and hung up, then did a White Pages Google search for Knowltons in Raleigh. There were two, a William and a Beverly. No Paul. Everett must have died. I entered William's number into my contacts.

A nap sounded pretty good so I lay down on the couch, surprised to wake up two hours later. It was too early for dinner, so I grabbed my gym bag and headed down to the club instead. If there wasn't a basketball game going on, at least I could lift some weights and sweat a bit in the steam room.

The parking lot of the Marin Gym and Spa was packed when I got there. Jaguars, Land Cruisers, Land Rovers, Lexuses and BMW SUVs. All with heavy-duty all-season tires to go with their four-wheel-drive transmissions. Perfect for Marin's freeways, mall parking lots, and suburban cul-de-sacs. And for all those times when it snowed in Tiburon.

I walked in just as an aerobics class was letting out. Some two dozen thirty-ish mothers sucking on bottled water or smoothies from the juice bar were picking up their toddlers in childcare. Most wore oversized gray t-shirts, black leggings to just below the knee, and expensive Nike cross-trainers. A lot of *very* nice calves.

I grabbed a locker and went upstairs to the basketball court—they reserve it for a couple of hours Friday afternoons for players 40 and older. A full-court five-on-five game was in full swing, with a couple of guys waiting for winners. Most of them I'd played with before. I nodded to Stan Harper, who took a pass, and sunk a three. I gave him a thumbs-up, added my name to the board, stretched a bit, and then shot some free throws on the side court to warm up.

Harper's team won, and stayed on the court. We needed two to flesh out our team, so the losers shot for the spots. I went over to Harper, who was toweling off.

"This what we pay our public servants to do?" I asked, bounce-passing him a ball.

He tossed his towel in the corner and grabbed the ball. "Late lunch, man. What're you doin'?"

"Just need to run," I said.

He nodded and sunk a jump shot from the sideline.

"Enough of that shit," I said.

He took a pass from someone under the hoop, and fired another jump shot. "Nothin' but net, as they say. Come on, chump."

The game began, and Harper was on fire. We played to 24, and Harper made over half of their points. We got eight. I got two. Fortunately, no one was waiting to play, so we ran it right back, coming a bit closer in the second game. We were just about to start a third when the door opened and a college girl in a Marin Gym and Spa t-shirt led a half dozen or so junior-high-age girls onto the court. "Four o'clock, guys," she said. "Sorry."

We caught our breath while she had them shoot around a bit, and then I followed Harper downstairs. "Steam?" he said, holding the locker-room door open for me.

"Sure, see you in there."

When I walked in the steam was so thick I could barely see. Harper was sitting on the higher tier, a towel around his waist. There was only one other guy in there.

"Mike," he said. "You know Brian Wolfe, don't you?"

I didn't.

"Brian Wolfe, Mike McMahon."

"Nice to meet you," I said.

"McMahon and I went to Drake High together."

"Really?" Wolfe said. "Probably played against you guys. I went to Tam."

"I thought all you guys did at Tam was smoke pot," Harper said.

"Didn't stop us from playing football," Wolfe said, standing and heading for the door. He pulled it open and said, "Don't waste away in there."

Harper laughed. "See you, man." Then he lay back on the tile, making a pillow out of his laced-together fingers. "So, McMahon. What's going on with the Jimmy Rooney thing?"

I told him a very abbreviated version of the last few days.

"You think he was murdered?"

I took a breath, got a big slug of steam, and coughed. "I don't know," I said. "I've found out some weird shit going on but I can't seem to make the pieces fit together."

"Yet."

"Yet."

"Knowing you, you'll pull it off."

"Besides, the coroner's report was pretty clear. Massive injuries from the crash, caused by cardiac arrest, given his medical history." Even my hair was getting hot now.

"But they're not absolutely certain it was cardiac arrest, right?"

"Right . . . I wonder if cardiac arrest can be induced."

"Ask Wolfe," Harper said. "If anyone'd know, he would."

"Wolfe?"

"He's a cardiologist. Up at Marin General. One of the best. You'd have recognized him if it weren't so steamy in here. You know those commercials? That's him getting handed the X-ray right when the voice-over starts."

"No shit," I said. "I should talk to him."

"I would."

"I'll see you," I said. "I'm going to try to catch him."

"Later."

I pulled the door open, followed a billow of steam out into the locker room, and looked around. Wolfe had already gone. Damn.

When I got home, I popped *Sandy Morning* into the CD player, played "Out on a Limb," and listened again, thinking about what Chet Porter had said.

All alone in a tree and out on a limb
Singing my song, hellbound by hymns
The leaves have all fallen, my song is undone
I'm bathed in the moonlight, an unfortunate son

— 14 —

Every so often I get the urge to play music on stage again. Actually, more than every so often. Usually when Becka and I are on the skids. When things are going well, she's about all I need. But when they're not, I tend to want to play music and drive fast. Dumb, I know, and I also know what Fruedians say about guitars and cars. Maybe there's something to it. Maybe not.

At any rate, when I got home from the gym, I ate a quick sandwich while I watched the news on CNN, then threw my Les Paul into the back of Portia and headed into San Francisco. I had a couple of Harps at O'Shannon's on Geary, where a button-accordion player was accompanying a punky tenor with pierces and tattoos on traditional Irish folk songs. I put a fiver in his tip jar, asked him to do "Danny Boy," and sat listening and thinking about Johnny Sands. When he finished, I gave him a thumbs-up, then left and drove down South of Market to Dinty's, where every Thursday night the house band, the Blue Jobs, hosts an open jam. Anyone who wants to can sit in for a couple of tunes, usually trading licks with their guitar player, a long-haired anemic-looking kid named Whitney, who plays a B.B. King-style Gibson and can rip it up just like the Blues Boy himself.

It was early, and the place was pretty empty. I set my guitar case up by the stage alongside three or four others, scribbled my name on the chalkboard, then went over to the bar and ordered a shot and a beer. Always like to loosen up a little. I listened to the music for a bit while I read the box scores in the sports section of the *Chronicle* and watched over my shoulder for the regulars—six or seven pretty decent players who showed up every week and jammed with the band for a few numbers. Some of them were actually pretty good, like Carlos, this little Mexican kid who lived over in the Mission and played Stevie Ray Vaughan-style on an old beat-up Melody Maker.

It was only 8:30, and typically nothing much happened till around 10, so I ordered another beer and found myself thinking again about Johnny Sands and Jim Rooney. So far the parts just weren't fitting together. I grabbed a bar napkin and jotted down a few notes, then turned it over and wrote down all the names even peripherally connected to the case: Jim and Sarah Rooney, Lester Corbin, Kevin Sands, Roger Sands, Mrs. Sands, Howard Silva, Ted Knowlton and Pedro Rodriguez, and Carla, Roger's mom. Not that many, once you put them down on paper. Ted Knowlton, mystery man. I figured I should call the number in Raleigh. Also that I should try to talk to Kevin. I drew lines connecting all the names on the napkin, based on whether they knew each other, hoping maybe I'd see something I hadn't thought of.

Not yet. At least not at 9:30 at night in a loud bar after three beers and a shot of Jameson's.

I wrote down Becka's name just for the hell of it.

The other mystery man, of course, was Howard Silva. How could I get a hold of him?

The Blue Jobs took a break, Whitney announcing that they'd be jamming the second set and working through the list on the chalkboard. My name was at the top. I went over and took my guitar out of the case, tuned, and stepped up on stage.

Whitney shook his hair out of his face, looked at me, and smiled. "E?"

I nodded and followed him deep into a twelve-bar blues.

He took the first break, then stepped back beside the bass player, and I took the second. Not a scorcher, but passable, and we got a decent round of applause. From there we went right into "Good Morning, Little School Girl" and then "Stormy Monday," everyone getting in at least one solo, even the drummer. Afterward, Whitney walked across the stage to me. "Hey, man, I forgot your name. Sorry."

I told him, and he announced it to the crowd, clearly indicating I was done, as another guy walked onstage with an old, dinged-up white Telecaster and plugged in. I put my guitar back in its case, hauled it over to the bar, and listened to a couple of more songs, then headed out into the night, caught Van Ness at Market and drove north out of the city, over the bridge.

It was after midnight when I got home. I poured a Jameson's, and turned on Conan and watched him patronize Lindsey Lohan for a few minutes, then called Becka.

"Jees, Mike, it's after twelve o'clock."

"You want to come over?"

"What?"

"You want to come over?"

She let out a breath. "I thought you finally understood. We're through. You find the—?"

"Yes, I found the key. I'm mailing it back to you tomorrow."

"Oh, Michael . . . "

"You don't even need it tonight. I'll leave the door unlocked. In fact, I'll wait for you outside."

"Michael, I'm not coming over. Maybe in a month, maybe in a couple of months we can take stock of things. But we . . . I really need to let it go for a while. I think you do too."

"Then you're not coming over?"

"I'm not coming over. Michael, goodnight. Go to bed. We'll talk another time."

She hung up then, and I woke up the next morning at 7:30 on the couch, thirsty and needing to piss.

I fixed a strong cup of coffee and drank it while I read the newspaper, then called the number I had for William Knowlton.

"This is Bill."

"Mr. Knowlton, this is Mike McMahon. I'm a private investigator out in California. I assume you've heard about Jim Rooney's death . . ."

"I read about it."

"His wife hired me look into it. She thinks there might be more to the accident."

"Like . . . ?

"Like maybe it wasn't an accident."

"Hmmm . . . That sounds pretty crazy to me."

"Maybe. But anyway I was hoping I might be able to talk to your brother. I understand he used to hang around with the band," I said.

"He and Johnny and Kevin grew up together."

"Uh huh. Lester Corbin told me he worked with the band, was a roadie or something, so he knew Jim Rooney too."

"Of course."

"Can you tell me how I might be able to get a hold of

your brother?"

There was a long pause.

"I'm sorry, Mr. Knowlton. I don't mean to take much of your time, but Lester Corbin told me Ted was with Johnny the night of the crash, and it looks like there might be a connection between Johnny's plane going down and Jimmy Rooney's death. Do you have a number where I could reach your brother?"

"Mr. McMahon. I saw my brother all of about three times between 1976 and when he moved to San Francisco in 1981. I never saw him after that. He died in 1984."

I was caught off guard. "Oh. I'm sorry. I didn't—"

"It's okay. Now, if you'll excuse me, I really have some things I must attend to."

"Sure, thanks. Sorry to bother you."

I hung up then, and took my coffee out onto the patio. Luther ambled over and put his head on my thigh and looked up at me with those big dark eyes. I finished my coffee, went inside and showered, then dressed and headed to the Marin County library. I had a hunch.

— 15 —

It didn't take me long to find what I was looking for. Theodore Knowlton died in San Francisco on April 12, 1984. He was thirty-five. He had worked in the city finance offices and had been active in several local organizations, including a bicycling club and Bay Area Watercolorists. He left a companion, Salvador Black. Donations were to be sent to the Gough Street AIDS Foundation.

Just what I thought.

I wondered if Black was still alive.

I drove home and picked up Luther, then drove out to Fort Cronkite, where I let him run in the waves for a half hour or so.

On my way home, I stopped at Nordstrom's to look for something for Becka. I needed some kind of peace offering. What did she need?

Oops.

Gift foul!

Women get pouty when you buy them what they need. Give me a gift I can use. New guitar strings, a garden hose, drill bits, a socket set, a six-pack, a leaf blower. Even a bag of treats for Luther. But I've learned. No useful stuff at all. Bath mats, shower curtains, microwaves, bread knives, salad spinners. Wonderful gifts by my reckoning. Not by hers. Although candlesticks have worked in a pinch. A sexy nightgown? Nope. *This is a gift for you, Michael,* she'd say. Not when things are going this badly.

A book? Perf . . . nah. She'd take it wrong. No matter what it was. *And what are you trying to tell me by this, Michael?*

Honey, it's just a book. I'm not trying to tell you anything at all.

Yeah, right. Pride and Prejudice? *Now I'm too proud?*

No, not at all . . .

Prejudiced?

Finally, I left and stopped at Keiko's, bought her a gift certificate for a massage, and had it sent anonymously.

When I got home I made two more lists of all the people I could think of who were connected to Jim Rooney. One for people I'd talked with and one for people I hadn't and might not even be able to. The "hadn't" list included Kevin of course, Silva, Rodriguez, Ted Knowlton, and Salvador Black. Knowlton and Rodriguez were out. Silva I didn't know if I'd be able to track down, and Sal Black, if he were alive, would probably be just as difficult. But I knew where Kevin Sands was. I'd known all along. I called and made an appointment with the resident physician for Monday.

I also still needed to talk to Brian Wolfe and whomever Jim Rooney had been working with at Narwhal Books.

— 16 —

Vineland Group Home is located about an hour north of San Francisco in the north end of the Napa Valley on the side of a rolling hill overlooking the little wine-country town of Calistoga, miles and miles of vineyards, and a dozen or so wineries. I'd seen the place from a distance many times over the years, as I'd wandered through the valley—often on Sunday-afternoon wine-tasting excursions with Becka—but had never actually driven up the quarter-mile winding road to the facility itself.

I left Mill Valley about 11 and headed up Highway 101, catching 37 east then 121 north at Sonoma Raceway—a sweet little two-and-a-half mile, 12-turn race course on the Sonoma County hillside—then cut over into the Napa Valley and stopped in St. Helena for lunch, parking on Main Street behind a gorgeous white Jaguar XK-8 convertible. My favorite cafe was packed, so I crossed the street to a little deli and bought a turkey sandwich and a split of chardonnay and had myself a little picnic on the lawn of a small park and watched the tourists walk by. When I got back to my car, a couple of high-school-age kids with skateboards and long sagging shorts and their hats on backwards were standing next to it.

They turned awkwardly when they saw me approaching and pretended like they hadn't been staring at it.

"You guys like Porsches?" I said, trying not to sound too patronizing.

They turned and shrugged. "Some of 'em," one said. "My dad collects 'em. He's got one of these '63s."

"Really?" I said, skeptical.

"Uh huh. They're pieces of shit, though."

"Really?" I said again.

"I'll take a '59 Speedster any day."

I nodded. "Nice cars. Your dad got one of them?"

"Two," he said. ""One's mine when I turn 18."

"Lucky you," I said.

They turned and walked away, tossed their skateboards into the back seat of the Jaguar, started it up, and gave me just a bit of tire squeal as they pulled out sharply in front of a dark blue Hundai. I got in my piece-of-shit car and headed up the road to Vineland where I had an appointment with Kevin's doctor at 1:30.

The private road up the hillside was lined with towering eucalyptus trees and old oleander just starting to bloom, making a vivid pattern of lavenders and whites between the eucalyptus, the roadside mulchy with peely bark and crunchy black pods. At the top of the hill, the road opened up to a large parking lot, where a sign pointed one way for staff and one way for visitors. I parked my piece-of-shit car and walked along a neat pathway lined with trailing rosemary and wild California poppies to the office. Inside, an all-string version of "Hey Jude" was playing softly from hidden speakers, and a couple of receptionists in white were hunched over some papers behind a desk. They looked up when I walked in.

"Can we help you?" one said, as they both tried to smile warmly.

"I have an appointment with Dr. Spencer," I said.

One of them slid a ledgerbook across the desk, set it on top of the papers, and with the eraser end of a pencil tracked the column to 1:30. "Yes . . . uh, Mr. McMahon, is it?"

I nodded.

The one who had been speaking looked at the other, who turned and disappeared through a side door.

"My name's Gretchen," she said. "Go ahead and sign in here. Dr. Spencer should be ready to see you in a few minutes. You can sit down if you'd like."

I thanked her and turned toward a couple of couches set across from each other, a coffee table between them on which a handful of magazines were neatly arranged. *Wine Spectator, Golf Digest, Psychology Today.* I wandered around the room, checking out the artwork on the walls, beautifully framed watercolor paintings of the various grapes grown in the area. Chardonnays, Cabernets, merlots, zinfandels, all hanging ripe on leafy vines. As if a Musak-y "Hey Jude" weren't bad enough, an all-string version of "Honky Tonk Women" came on. Thankfully, Gretchen's phone rang, and she called my name before I had a chance to get ill.

"Follow me," she said, standing and walking over to the side door.

She led me down a long, sterile hallway lined with oversized photos of benefactors and past administrators, then stopped at an open door and let me walk in ahead of her.

Dr. Spencer was sitting in a large black-leather chair behind a football-field-sized walnut desk, almost bare except for a thick file, an open medical journal turned over to mark his place, a leather dice cup holding an assortment of pencils and pens, and a brass paperweight in the form of a golf ball with two crossed clubs on top.

"Dr. Spencer, this is Mr. McMahon."

He stood and extended his hand over his desk, and we shook. "Mr. McMahon, nice to meet you. Sit down. Thanks, Gretchen."

I sat in a chrome and fabric chair in front of Spencer's desk. Neither of us spoke as we waited for her to leave and walk back down the hallway. I looked at the framed diplomas on the wall and the prints of past Napa Valley Mustard Festivals. Then Spencer walked around to the side of his desk and stood before a large window looking out. He was younger than I'd expected him to be. Barely forty, I guessed, baby-faced, pasty, a little puffy, his thin hair already receding. He wore a light brown suit vest and slacks, the jacket hanging on a coat rack in the corner. The sleeves of his white shirt were rolled up to the elbow. He turned and half sat on the edge of his desk in front of me.

"Kevin Sands," he said, nodding thoughtfully and staring past me at the wall. He laughed softly and shook his head. "Fascinating case."

I waited for him to continue, but he snapped out of it, and looked at me. "You said on the phone you're a private investigator?"

"That's right," I said, reaching for my wallet for a business card, which I handed to him.

He looked at it briefly, nodded, then set it on his desk. "And you want to talk to him?"

"I do. He's sort of an indirect connection to a case I'm working on. You don't remember a Jim Rooney, do you? Killed in a car accident out by Stinson Beach a couple of months ago?"

"Mr. McMahon," Spencer said, standing and walking back around his desk to his chair. "I keep very close tabs on our residents." He put his hands on the back of the chair, then sat down and picked up the file. "See this? This contains not only Kevin's medical history but anything and everything about it that might even be remotely connected." He thumbed through it briefly, then pulled out a newspaper clipping and held it up to me. "MUSICIAN KILLED IN HIGHWAY 1 CRASH." He continued: "Since there's so much we can't know in this business, I try to know everything about what I can." He paused, pulled a pencil out of a coffee cup and tapped it on the desk. "Let's see, Jim Rooney, drummer for the Johnny Sands Band, went to high school with Johnny and Kevin, played in several jazz bands in the '80s, cut a couple of albums. Wife, Sarah. No kids. Am I close?"

"Impressive," I said. "So much for the background I thought I was going to have to give you."

"So what's your part in this?"

"Sarah thinks Jim might have been murdered."

Spencer nodded, not seeming to be fazed, then looked at me to continue.

I told him about Rooney's book deal and the missing manuscript.

He listened thoughtfully. "I assume you've got more than that?"

"Not much more, but yeah, enough to, well, keep me interested."

Spencer looked at me and bit his lower lip. "Mr. McMahon, I really doubt you're going to get much out of Kevin. He's been here for close to thirty years. Even if he had something, I don't know what you could do with it. Certainly not much in court."

"I know," I said, "but I think there may be connections between Jim's death and Johnny's. I'd just like to talk to him, feel him out."

He tapped the pencil, then got suddenly serious and took a deep breath. "Mr. McMahon, how much do you know about schizophrenia?"

I shrugged. "Not much. I've done a little reading on line, but it's pretty general. Lots of different types, and things that can bring it on, I guess."

"That's right. There are many different types, though most usually manifest themselves in the late teens or early adulthood." He stroked his chin thoughtfully. "Now, Kevin, he's hard to classify. Sometimes he just seems hebephrenic, disorganized, mildly hallucinatory. Then sometimes he's nearly catatonic, although we can usually see that coming. Excitability, impulsiveness, and then, then nothing. He becomes mute and nearly immobile. Sometimes for hours."

"Genetic? Environmental?" I asked.

"Who knows?" Spencer said, sighing. "There's a new study every month, but nothing conclusive. Most research these days suggests genetics does play a role of some kind, but what we're really looking at is biochemical abnormalities in the brain. Environment, stressful periods, trauma may trigger it." He turned up his hands.

"Drugs?" I asked.

"Oh, we use a range of various anti-psychotics?"

"I mean can drugs trigger it?"

"Oh, sure, almost anything can, depending on the degree to which the individual interprets that experience as traumatic. But there is one big misconception. Just doing too many drugs is most likely not going to bring about schizophrenia. It's like a time bomb ticking away. You know, you hear about these guys, Kevin's age a lot of them, 'Too many drugs,' they say, 'Too much LSD.' Not likely. Remember, roughly eight in a thousand people are going to develop schizophrenia in their lifetimes, and that number hasn't really changed much over the years."

He leaned back in his chair, laced his hands behind his head. "No, it's more likely something traumatic triggered it. Oh, he may have done drugs, but research just doesn't support that that would trigger it."

"The plane crash?"

"Very possible, but again, who knows?"

"Right," I said.

"And the thing is, it's not going away," Spencer said. "Something like thirty percent of schizophrenics recover, at least enough to function in the world, but not Kevin." He leaned forward, stood, went to the window and looked out. "He's been doing pretty well these days, though." He turned to look at me. "That's why I said to come on up. But I can't promise anything. And tread gently."

"Of course."

"Shall we?"

I nodded.

"Follow me." He walked to the door and stood beside it, indicating for me to lead the way. "Down the hall to the right," he said.

I walked down a short hallway, at the end of which a large glass door opened up onto a lawn and patio surrounded by six or eight small gray duplexes. He caught up to me and pushed the door open ahead of me. I stopped when I got outside the door. He let it close and stood beside me. "Beautiful, isn't it?" he said.

The patio—made of square-foot terra-cotta tiles—stretched out for fifty feet or so, then met the lawn, which rolled out and off the hillside. Magnificent oaks, their large branches greened with moss, were scattered about the lawn, in the middle of which was a huge fountain that looked like it had come straight from fourth-century-BC Greece, water pouring from an urn held by a woman whose drape wrapped her waist and legs.

"Come on." Spencer led me around the side of the building, where the lawn gave way to a garden of hydrangeas, Japanese maples, a sprawling deep green periwinkle groundcover, and a handful of concrete benches set among the gravel pathways. At one, a man sat hunched over a guitar.

"Kevin Sands," Spencer said.

I took a step forward, but Spencer put his hand on my shoulder. "Not yet," he said. "Hang on." He put his finger to lips. "Listen."

I turned back to Kevin and held my breath. He was playing music unlike anything I'd ever heard. Some kind of open tuning that made the guitar sound something like a cross between a harp and a Hawaiian slack-key guitar, the deep fullness from the Martin dreadnaught an unearthly soundtrack to the quiet garden scene.

"He doesn't seem too bad off," I said, "at least from my medically naive point of view."

Spencer nodded, looked at me and smiled. "Meds."

We listened for a few more minutes. Spencer watched closely, seeming to take mental notes, then said, "Wait here," and walked slowly over to the bench where Kevin was sitting. Kevin looked up, stopped playing, and Spencer sat down beside him. They spoke for a few moments, Spencer nodding, Kevin looking away. Then Spencer looked up at me and signaled for me to come over.

Kevin set his guitar across his lap as I approached him, smiled quickly, then reached for a pack of cigarettes on the bench beside him and lit one. He looked down, then up at me, his eyes darting. I'd read so much about Brian Wilson, nearly catatonic, his baby grand set in a sand box in his Malibu mansion so he could play with his toes in the sand, that I guess I was expecting Kevin to be much more of a basket case than he seemed to be. What did catch me off guard, though, was how old he looked. I'd known he'd be in his mid-sixties, but in my mind's eye he was still that kid on the cover of all those Johnny Sands Band albums. He wore wire-rim glasses and a graying mustache, and just a circlet of gray hair and a thin wisp of a ponytail on his otherwise bald pate. Only his skin looked young, reflecting the thirty years in the institution.

"Kevin," Spencer said, "this is Mike McMahon. Mike, Kevin Sands."

We shook hands, Kevin letting the cigarette burn from the corner of his mouth. I looked at Spencer, who shrugged as if to indicate that everything was okay. Kevin picked the guitar back up, strummed a minor discordant chord, let it ring, then set the instrument down, leaning it against the front of the bench.

"That was a beautiful piece you were playing a few minutes ago," I said. "What's that tuning."

Kevin took a pull on his cigarette, blew the smoke up into the air above his head, and nodded. "Dadgad," he said. He picked the guitar back up and strummed it a string at a time. D-A-D-G-A-D. It was a classic tuning used by traditional Irish players.

Kevin set the guitar back down. "You want a smoke? I know he don't." Spoken like a Raleigh good ol' boy.

"No thanks," I said. "I would like to ask you a couple of questions, though."

Kevin took another drag on his cigarette and rested his other hand on his guitar, tapping nervously.

I caught Spencer's eye. He was indicating that I should take it easy.

"That okay, Kevin?" Spencer said.

"Sure, man."

"Actually," I started, "I'm a musician myself, and—"

He shook his head rhythmically from side to side, then leaned back against the bench and took a long breath, holding his cigarette in front of his face and watching it burn down.

"I was hoping you could tell me a little about your last concert."

Kevin took a breath. "Like all of them," he said. "Hour-long set, ten-minute break, another half hour, encore "Out on a Limb.""

"And then?"

"Back stage to unwind."

I looked to Spencer, then back at Kevin. "And then you were planning to fly back to Raleigh?"

Bad call. Kevin was clearly upset. "Fuck," he said, then took several deep breaths. Spencer cringed.

Kevin regained his composure. "Just wanted to go back to Raleigh to be with my girlfriend for a few days between shows. Woulda been me. Shoulda been me."

"You okay?" I said.

He took another deep breath, nodded. "My brother insisted. Our manager and me argued with him, but he insisted. I thought he was going to have a shit-fit, he was so upset. I'd never seen my brother so stuck on something. Finally, he just bailed, left with the pilot. Our manager was running after them. Crazy. We never saw him again. Them."

Spencer gave me the tread-gently look.

"Did your brother say why he wanted to go back to Raleigh?"

Kevin shook his head, looked up at sky.

Spencer put his hand on Kevin's shoulder.

I wanted to ask him about Roger, but it didn't seem like a good time.

Spencer looked at me, then back at Kevin. "Kevin, Mr. McMahon and I are going back to my office now, but Mr. McMahon would like to talk with you . . . another time?" He looked at me. I nodded. "So I'm going to make arrangements for him to come back."

Kevin dropped his cigarette in the gravel, ground it out with the toe of his shoe, and lit another.

"That okay with you?"

Kevin nodded, then picked up his guitar and strummed it softly.

Spencer took me by the elbow. "Come on," he said. "Now's

not good."

I looked at Kevin, hunched over his guitar, fingerpicking a slow, dirgy "Minstrel Boy," an old Irish ballad. "Nice to meet you," I said.

Kevin nodded without looking up, slid his hand up the fretboard and began playing the song an octave higher.

"Come on," Spencer said again. "Let's go back to the office."

As we walked away, Kevin segued from "Minstrel Boy" into "Danny Boy." I could barely hear, "The pipes, the pipes are calling."

When we got to Spencer's office door, he stopped, turned to me, and shook his head. "Sorry," he said, then seemed to be at a loss for words. "Maybe try again next week?"

"Sure," I said. "No problem."

"Can you find your way out of here?"

"Sure," I said again, "down the hall here, right?"

My phone buzzed as I was heading back through St. Helena. I recognized the number on my screen. Vineland.

"This is Mike," I said.

It was Spencer. "Mr. McMahon," he said. "Listen," he said. "We don't have much call for security up here, but we do have a cam going 24/7 in the lobby. My staff tells me a couple of guys were in day before yesterday asking to see Kevin. They told 'em no. They left. But we got it on tape."

"You seen it?"

"Not yet," he said, "but I was hoping you might be able to come back up tomorrow. We'll take a look at it together, and then if Kevin's up to it maybe we could try to talk to him again."

"Sure. What time?"

"First thing? Eight-thirty?"

"See you then," I said.

My head wasn't completely in class that night, but I managed to fake it. Most of the material I knew like the back of my band. The San Francisco music scene from 1965 to the early '70s. The Grateful Dead, Jefferson Airplane, Quicksilver, Big Brother, Moby Grape, Blue Cheer, the Beau Brummels, the Charlatans, the Sons of Champlain, Sly, Santana. Most of the students had at least heard of the bands we talked about, though Chet Porter was the only one who knew the Flaming Groovies and the Great Society. I was just about to dismiss them a half hour early when Shelley Martin raised her hand.

"Shelley?"

"What about the Ace of Cups?"

She had me there. The Ace of Cups was the only successful all-women rock band back in a time when the genre was dominated by men, except of course for Grace Slick and Janis Joplin, and had recently reunited to record and perform together. I let Shelley play a YouTube clip that was a montage of footage from a show at the Mt. Tam amphitheater in 1967 and footage from the last couple of years. They still rocked. And they still looked really good. Shelley kind of drove me crazy, but, well, it was the highlight of that night's class. I thanked her, and she bowed to me, her palms pressed together at her chest.

After class I stopped in at the Owl for a quick Jameson's, and when I got home did some more reading on schizophrenia, most of the articles just recycling each other's information. I kept coming back to trauma. Of course, it seemed, a brother's death in plane crash could be traumatic, even more so if you were supposed to be the one on the plane.

— 17 —

When I arrived at Vineland the next morning, Gretchen met me at the door and led me directly down the hall to a small conference room with a large table, a dozen or so chairs, and a stand with a flat-screen television hooked up to a computer. "Sit down," she said. "Dr. Spencer will be here in a moment."

She turned to leave, almost bumping into Spencer as he walked through the door.

"McMahon," he said, "thanks for coming." He walked over to the video monitor, grabbed the remote from on top of it, then sat down across the table from me. "Like I told you on the phone, I don't know what the hell's going on around here." He turned his palms up. "Kevin doesn't get many visitors. His mom used to come up pretty regularly but hasn't been around much lately, and a woman named Carla, I guess she would've been his sister-in-law if Johnny hadn't died, comes by twice a year or so, but that's it, in the ten years I've been here."

He pointed the remote at the monitor, turned it on, then started the video. "Okay," he said, "watch closely. You'll see them walk in."

The screen showed an empty lobby.

"Now, here," Spencer said.

The double automatic doors opened and two men walked in.

"Son of a bitch," I said.

"What?" Spencer said, pressing "Pause." "You know them?"

"I don't know who the older guy is but the younger one's Roger Sands, Kevin's nephew."

The image on the screen was still, Roger's face frozen in a digital smirk.

"Roger Sands?" Spencer said, mostly under his breath.

I nodded. "Roger Sands."

"And you don't know the other guy?"

"No idea," I said.

Spencer pointed the remote at the monitor and shut it off. "There's not much after this," he said. "The camera loses them." He leaned back in his chair and crossed his arms. "Roger Sands," he said. "What do you think he could be doing in town? He lives down south, doesn't he?"

"Yep," I said, nodding. "And says he never gets up this way."

"You've talked to him?"

"Sure," I said, "though I don't know how honest he was being with me. He's also been in touch with Lester Corbin and Sarah Rooney."

"I'd sure like to find out who that other guy is."

"So would I," I said. "In fact, I've got an idea. Can you download that footage and send it to me?"

"How 'bout if I just get some stills printed up? I'll get the best shots of Mystery Man there and have some prints made. That work? We can scan them in right now and you can take them with you."

I drove back to Mill Valley with four photos on the seat beside me. Spencer had found a pretty clear frame that showed both of them from the front. I glanced at it from time to time as I drove, appreciating the irony. Roger Sands, finally in a starring role. But who was the co-star? I made a mental list of the people I'd show it to, starting with Sarah Rooney.

I also wanted to talk again with Roger Sands. Although I doubted that I'd find him at the Casas Del Sol townhouses, number 146B.

Spencer called back the next morning. Shortly after midnight, an aide at Vineland had heard a gagging sound coming from Kevin Sands' room. She knocked, then let herself in and found him sitting upright in his bed gasping for air, his pillow on the floor. The sliding-glass door to the patio was open. Someone had broken in and tried to suffocate him with his pillow. It looked like whoever it was had panicked when Kevin started making noise. Kevin only saw his attacker's back as he ran through the patio door.

Kevin would be fine, Spencer told me, although they'd had to increase his medication and he wouldn't be able to see me again for a few days at best. The Napa County Sheriff's department had the video of Kevin's two would-be visitors and would probably be contacting me.

I decided to save them the trouble, but called Harper first. I gave him the basic details and then asked him if he knew anyone who worked for the Napa County Sheriff I could talk to.

"'Anyone'?" he said. "Sure, I think I know 'em all. Good group of guys. Pretty slow up there. This'll be big."

"Can they handle it?"

"Oh, sure. I don't know if they'll find the guy. But they'll do everything right trying to. Talk to Owens. Jerry Owens. He's a deputy. We met at a conference in Vegas ten or twelve years ago."

I thanked him and phoned the Napa Valley Sheriff. Deputy Owens wasn't in, but I got through to his voice mail and left a message, mentioning that I'd just talked with Harper. He called me back an hour later.

Jerry Owens knew about the case and had already met with the deputies who'd responded to the 9-1-1 call. He'd also downloaded the video. He wanted to talk to me about Roger and whoever was with him at Vineland.

I made an appointment for the first thing the next morning. In the meantime, I scanned copies of the best photo and emailed one to Lester Corbin and one to Mrs. Sands. Then I phoned Sarah Rooney and asked her to meet me for lunch.

We met at Zeek's in Sausalito and were given a table on the back deck overlooking the water. I pulled out the photo as soon as we sat down. Sarah caught her breath, then bent over the photo looking at it closely. Then she sat back shaking her head.

"Well?" I said, impatiently. "You know who that is with Roger?"

She closed her eyes and put her fingers to her cheeks. "My meter reader," she said, opening her eyes again and looking out to the bay.

"Your *meter reader*?"

"My meter reader. He stopped by the house a couple of weeks ago and said he was there to check my utilities meters which he said didn't seem to be getting an accurate reading. Then said I could switch over to some special rate if I planned to be gone more than a few days a month. All he needed to know was the approximate dates I'd be gone."

I took a breath.

"Seemed legit to me. I couldn't have known he wasn't from Pacific Gas and Utilities."

"What'd you tell him?"

"That I hadn't been away and that I wasn't planning on going away."

"Good, I guess."

She shook her head slowly. "Funny thing, too. Not from around here. In fact, he sounded like Jim would when he was tired. Definitely from somewhere in the south." She paused. "Should I go stay with one of my sisters, Mike? One's up in Sebastopol. I'm kinda creeped out by all this."

"Guess it couldn't hurt," I said. "I doubt you're in any danger, but as long as you've got a place. In fact, you might take someone with you when you go get your stuff."

"My sister's husband."

"Perfect," I said.

Our lunches arrived, and we ate quickly, Sarah clearly anxious. Understandably.

"Go ahead," I said. "You need to get going."

She picked her purse up off the deck. "Okay," she said, stood and headed out to the parking lot.

The waitress came, I signed for lunch, and headed back to my place.

— 18 —

I hadn't been home ten minutes when my phone buzzed. Becka. I let her leave a voice mail, grabbed a beer out of the refrigerator, and let Luther in. "Thanks, Michael. That was sweet. It isn't going to work, though. Not this time. In fact, I'm going to Tahoe for a couple of days with a friend. Hope you're doing okay."

A "*friend*"? Going to Tahoe with a "*friend*"? Had to be Lawrence Lundford, the arrogant little linguist with the office down the hall from hers.

I took a deep breath and a long pull on my beer. This hurt.

I started to call her, stopped after hitting the first six numbers, put my phone on the counter, then picked it up again, hit all seven.

"Hello?"

"Lawrence Lundford? You're going out with Lawrence Lundford?"

"Michael! Don't be a baby."

"How long have you been seeing him?"

"I'm not *seeing* him. We're just friends, but he's been patient. We're just going up for a couple of days. It's our spring break, remember. Objections, your honor?"

Her spring break. I'd totally forgotten. I couldn't think of anything to say.

"You had your chance, Romeo."

"But I was thinking maybe we could go to a Giants' game tomorrow." I was desperate.

She laughed. "They're not in town."

I struggled for something to say. "I know. We could fly to Chicago."

"Michael, I've got plans. Now, was there something else?"

"No."

"Good-bye, Michael."

"Have a good time," I said, but I don't think she heard me.

Things were happening fast on the Rooney case, and I was becoming more and more convinced that he'd been murdered. I sat down at my computer, opened a Word document and entered everything I had trying to make sense of it all. In a nut shell. A very small nutshell. Here's what I had:

* Jim Rooney dead in car crash, probably not accidental.
* Pedro Rodriguez, witness to crash, dead, possibly murdered.
* Johnny Sands killed in plane crash in 1976.
* Brother Kevin institutionalized shortly after.
* Son Roger now living in LA, appearing in lives of Kevin, Lester Corbin, Sarah Rooney.
* Roger and mystery man visit Vineland.
* Attempt on Kevin's life.
* Mystery man in video shows up in meter-reader disguise at Sarah's house.
* Royalties from songs, way less than they should be.
* Book manuscript and electronic files missing.
* Ted Knowlton dead of AIDS.

What did it all mean? What could Jim have known that someone wouldn't want published, and who was that someone? And how did Jim actually die?

I shut off the computer, grabbed a sweatshirt, and took Luther for a midnight walk. The moon was full and hovering over the bay like a gigantic eyeball. The streets of Mill Valley were quiet, and even with old buddy Luther there I felt awfully alone. Becka and Lawrence Lundford! I put off going home for a long time, and when I finally did I took a big pull of Jameson's from the bottle to help me sleep.

I awoke about 8:30 to my phone's buzzing. I picked it up off the nightstand without sitting up, my head not clear enough to assume it was a robo call.

"This is Mike."

"Mr. McMahon, my name's Carla de Souza." She paused. "I'd like to meet with you if possible."

"Can I ask what this might be about?"

She hesitated. "Well, it's about . . . my son."

A runaway, no doubt. "Uh, Mrs. de Souza. I appreciate your thinking of me, but I'm not taking any new cases right now. I'd suggest—"

She cut me off. "Mr. McMahon, my son is Roger Sands. Your friend Stan Harper suggested I contact you."

I sat up suddenly. Carla! Of course. Spencer had mentioned her. "Oh," I said, trying to clear my head. "Yes, well, I'd love to meet you. Where? When?"

"I'm staying at the Embassy Suites in San Rafael. I don't know my way around the Bay Area very well. Can you come by the hotel?

"Of course, when?"

She paused for a moment. "Well, I'm only going to be in town until tomorrow."

"This morning?"

"Sure," she said.

"I'm on my way. Give me about an hour. Meet you in the restaurant there? I'll buy you coffee."

I showered and was out of the house in half an hour.

I took Carla de Souza to be the only woman sitting alone in the mostly empty restaurant, and the hostess confirmed. "You must be Mr. McMahon . . . Follow me." I sat down across from Mrs. de Souza as the waitress appeared with a water pitcher, filling my glass.

"Coffee?"

I nodded, turning my cup over.

Mrs. de Souza smiled at me. She was a tall thin woman in her mid-sixties, dark complected, her black hair graying and cut short, bangs hanging down almost to her piercing brown eyes. Her skin was leathered but she looked good, outdoorsy. Her white v-neck cotton sweater accented her dark skin, and her calf-length denim skirt was slit up past the knee. Small silver earrings in the shape of narrow feathers danced against her neck.

"Thanks for coming," she said, extending her hand. "I'm Carla. Sorry about the short notice." There it was again. Raleigh.

The waitress appeared and poured my coffee and topped off Carla's.

I felt like I had a million questions to ask her, but since she'd caught me off guard I wasn't sure where to start. "How'd you know to get a hold of me?" I asked.

She smiled and tore open a packet of sugar and poured it into her coffee, then stirred it slowly. "I know about the book," she said. "Jimmy Rooney had been trying to get a hold of me for the last two years. He wanted to interview me for it. I didn't want any part." She lifted her cup to her lips and took a sip. "Ooh . . . hot."

"Why not?"

She set her cup down and shook her head slightly. "Because there were things I didn't want to talk about. And I knew he would."

I poured some half and half into my coffee and waited for her to continue.

"Anyway, when I heard he'd died, I suspected there was more to it. And, well, I've been trying to figure out what to do. I finally got up the nerve to email the Marin County Sheriff's office, and I got a call last week from your friend Harper, who told me that as far as he was concerned the case was closed but that you were working on it."

I nodded. I wondered how much of what she didn't want to tell Jimmy Rooney she'd tell me.

She looked at me, then set her coffee cup down, both hands cradling it on the table, as though she were warming them. "This is hard," she said. "Harder even than I thought it would be."

I smiled awkwardly, trying to make her feel comfortable. "You said you wanted to talk about Roger."

She nodded slightly, staring down into her coffee, then looked up.

"Must've been hard to raise a son by yourself?"

She looked past me, then off toward a window. "I assume you know about Kevin."

"Yeah," I said. "I understand he's going to be okay, though."

"Okay?"

"His doctor told me they'd have to increase his medication for a few weeks, but he's going to be fine."

She looked at me as though she had no idea what I was talking about.

"You said you assumed I knew about Kevin," I said.

She started to speak, but stopped as the waitress appeared and filled our cups. She reached up and played with one of her earrings.

The waitress stood beside the table, her notepad in hand.

"I'm just going to have coffee," Carla said.

The waitress looked at me.

I ordered a glass of orange juice and an onion bagel.

The waitress scribbled onto the pad and turned away.

Carla looked at me, eyes wide, whispered, "What happened to Kevin?"

I told her the story, as much as I knew, including the part about the video. She sat listening, rapt, unbelieving. When I finished, she shook her head. "Roger was with some guy at Vineland?"

"That footage is pretty clear."

"Why?"

"The million-dollar question," I said.

"And then someone tried to kill Kevin?"

"Apparently."

"But he's going to be okay?"

"That's what Dr. Spencer says."

"Thank goodness." She looked away for a moment then back at me. "That explains it, though," she said.

"Explains it?"

"Why they wouldn't let me see him."

"You drove up there?"

She nodded. "I fly up once or twice a year, rent a car, stay here, usually, and try to spend a couple of hours with him. Not this time. They wouldn't let me see him and wouldn't say why." She took another deep breath. "I can't believe someone tried to kill him. Why?"

"That's what I'd like to know," I said. "And maybe more about Roger."

She shook her head. "It's been so hard, watching him. He could have done anything he wanted but he . . . " She trailed off. "Probably my fault. I was never very good at discipline or setting boundaries. Actually, he's a very kind man, very loving, just never really had much in the way of direction."

The waitress set my orange juice and bagel on the table in front of me, tore a page from her note pad, and slipped a corner of it under my saucer, face down, then turned to another table.

"Carla took a deep breath. "Sorry." She bit her upper lip. "Mr. McMahon . . . "

"Mike."

"Roger is . . . well, how do I put this? Johnny wasn't Roger's dad." She looked away. "Kevin was . . . is."

"What?" I couldn't believe what I was hearing. "*Kevin*?"

She smiled. "Oh, yes. Kevin. Roger Sands' father is Kevin

Sands, not Johnny Sands . . . I would know."

I sat back in my chair and crossed my arms, trying to gather my thoughts.

"And that would have come out in Jim Rooney's book?"

She nodded. "Probably."

I spread some cream cheese on my bagel and took a bite. "I don't get it," I said. "Why . . . "

"Mr. McMahon, it's complicated. *Very* complicated. In fact, it's a real mess is what it is." She took a sip of her coffee. "Cooler now."

I let her continue.

"It doesn't make it any easier that my son's more or less thrown his life away."

"Who knows?" I said. "Besides you and Kevin."

"I'm not sure," she said. "Not too many. The guys in the band knew, of course. Jimmy, but . . . "

I nodded. "Anyone else? Their parents?"

She shook her head. "Nope. The only other person who knew was their manager."

"Howard Silva?"

She set her coffee cup down and tapped her lips with her forefingers. "Howard Silva. He knew everything. He decided everything."

"What ever happened to him?"

She shook her head. "No idea." Then, "You probably know by now that Kevin was supposed to be on that plane that night, not Johnny."

I nodded. "Lester Corbin told me. Any idea why they traded places?"

She shook her head. "None. I was just excited that Kevin was coming back to Raleigh for a few days. I missed him when they were on tour."

"I'll bet. You never traveled with them?"

She shook her head again.

"Roger and I were living with my parents. It was hard for them, but they were pretty understanding, considering."

"Whatever happened to them?"

"They both died young, in their sixties. Lester still out in in Santa Fe?"

"Still runnin' the little bed and breakfast."

She smiled. "I always really liked him . . . But here's the thing," she said. "When Johnny died . . . I mean, there should've been some money from those records. They were huge sellers. *Huge.* So Roger and I should have been the beneficiaries, even though he and I weren't married. Along with Johnny's mom. But the courts awarded her a bit and me just enough to keep Roger fed and in school clothes. Don't get me wrong. I'm not saying I ever wanted the money, especially since it wasn't rightfully mine, but it's always seemed weird to me that there wasn't more."

It did seem odd. At least five or six of the songs had been recorded over the years by well-known artists and been major hits a second time.

"There must be," I said. "Some of those songs have been covered almost as many times as 'White Christmas' and 'Yesterday.'"

"Exactly." She squinted. "I don't know much about it but isn't that what ASCAP and BMI do? Distribute money to the original artists?"

"Assuming the artists or the artists' beneficiaries own the rights."

She nodded. "God, we were so young, we didn't know anything about any of that. Just that Johnny wrote songs that sold lots of records."

"I assume there wasn't a will or anything . . . ?"

"We were 22, 23. Who makes a will when they're 22 or 23?"

"Listen," I said. "I know you said you were only going to be in town until tomorrow. But . . . " I looked at my watch. "This changes everything. I mean, I think."

— 19 —

Carla and I talked for another half hour or so. She told me that she couldn't extend her stay but she did say that I could phone her another time and we could talk more. She was living alone out in the desert near Palm Springs, had been for the last four years. Said she hardly ever left except to fly up to see Kevin.

When I got home, I put on *Sandy Morning,* lay back on the couch, and listened. When I got to "Out on a Limb," I played it back, again, then again. And I thought about what Chet Porter had said: *Could Johnny Sands have been gay?*

"*Out* on a limb . . . ?" Kind of a stretch. Maybe not. "Hellbound by *hymns.*" Hellbound by *hims. An unfortunate son.* And then there was Ted Knowlton, Johnny's friend and band groupie. Dead of AIDS. Not only was Porter probably right about Johnny Sands' being gay, but about his trying to tell the world about it in his songs.

Okay. Start over. New information, new questions:

* Roger Sands is the son of Kevin, not Johnny Sands.
* Johnny Sands, gay. Mid-1970s. The south.
* Jim Rooney's book would probably have disclosed both those things.
* How much did Roger know?

I had to try to track Roger down again. I also wanted to talk again with Mrs. Sands, in Phoenix. And to find Sal Black, Knowlton's partner. If he were still alive.

I figured I owed Sarah Rooney an update, so I called her and made an appointment to meet for dinner. Again.

"He was probably *what?* Sarah said incredulously, looking over the top of her glass of chardonnay. "I can't believe it."

We had just ordered fish and chips at the Marin Brewing Company and were sitting at a patio table outside.

I shrugged. "And I think your husband knew."

"Wait a minute," she said, "let me get this straight."

"So to speak," I said, smiling.

"Ha! Very funny . . . You're saying one of the most popular sex symbols of the 1970s was gay?"

"It's happened before."

She nodded.

"It's possible that he wasn't," I said, "but it sure seems like it." I told her about Ted Knowlton and quoted some song lyrics, but she didn't seem all that convinced. "Is there anything at all that your husband might have said over the years that would suggest he knew?"

She set her wine glass down and shook her head. "I mean, I know it doesn't mean all that much," she said, "but he did have a kid after all. Roger."

"Well . . . " I said. "I met with Roger's mom this morning."

"Really?" she said. "And . . . ?"

"And she told me—you ready for this?—that Roger's father is Kevin, not Johnny."

"What?"

"Kevin is Roger's father. According to his mom."

The waiter brought our dinners, and I took a bite of a chip, then poured some malt vinegar on my fish.

Sarah took a sip of wine, then looked away. "You believe her?"

"I do."

"You think Jimmy knew about that too?"

I nodded. "According to Carla."

"Wow. He never said anything."

"That's what I figured."

"And you think that's why someone killed him?"

"I think that might be part of it," I said, "but I also think there's more. It just doesn't seem like enough."

I took a bite of fish, washed it down with a swallow of beer. "I've got to talk to Roger again," I said. "I need to figure out why he paid that visit to Uncle Kevin slash his dad. Maybe twice."

She took a deep breath. She hadn't touched her meal.

"Gonna eat?" I said.

She nodded, picked up a piece of fish and nibbled on it, then dropped it back into the red, waxed-paper-lined plastic basket.

I finished mine, and watched her, taking a small bite now and then but mostly lost in thought. At one point, she excused herself and went upstairs to the restroom, returned a few minutes later looking more composed, but never did eat much of her dinner. Afterwards, I walked her to her car and stood in the parking lot watching her drive away. I wondered if maybe I should have waited until I had more before I told her what little I knew. Oh, well. Too late now.

I drove home hoping Becka would call.

I sat down in the living room with a beer and flipped on the television with the remote and watched the end of a Giants-Cubs game. The Giants won 6-2, increasing their winning streak to seven games. During the post-game wrap-up they talked about the reliever Juan Belmontez—22-year-old from the Dominican Republic they'd just called up from Triple-A. Afterward, I watched an old episode of the *Dick Van Dyke Show* on YouTube. Laura's big toe was stuck in a faucet in a hotel bathroom and Rob was trying to break down the door to help her.

I looked at the clock. Eleven. Too late to call most people, but not my good buddy Roger Sands. Mr. Night Owl himself.

To my surprise, he answered right away, said he recognized my number.

"Listen," I said, "I'd like to talk to you again. I don't know if this is a good time or—"

"I would like to talk to you," he said, "but this isn't the best time."

I could hear a woman in the background. "Who is it, Rog?"

"Can you call me tomorrow?" he said. "I just got in." Then to his friend: "Just a minute, Babe." He spoke again to me. "In the afternoon?"

"Sure," I said, "no problem." Then, on a lark, I added, "I need to know what you were doing up at Vineland Group Home."

There was a silence, then he spoke again to his friend, "Get yourself a drink. I'll be right there."

"I'll call you tomorrow," I said.

"Wait—" he began.

But I hit End Call, hoping my suggestion would negatively preoccupy him during his little rendezvous.

He called me back shortly after nine the next morning. A brand new tack. "Now, what was this about a group home?"

I wished I could have seen his lying face.

"Surveillance cam, dude. You're all over it."

There was a long pause, then a sigh. "I wanted to talk to Uncle Kevin."

"Uh huh."

"I mean, no big deal. Shit, I even told you, I'm thinking about recording some of my dad's songs. I just wanted to get his take on it, that's all. But they wouldn't even let me see him."

"Someone got in to see him," I said.

"What do you mean?"

"Someone tried to kill him."

"What? You're shitting me, man. Tried to kill him? Why? How?"

I told him the story.

"He going to be okay?"

"Yeah, he's going to be fine."

"At least that's good news."

I paused a moment, then said, "Roger, you've got to tell me one thing: Who was with you when you went up to Vineland to see your uncle?"

He didn't answer right away.

"This dude I met who wants to produce my CD. Said he wanted to meet Uncle Kevin."

"And that dude's name would be?"

"Peter Stern."

"You flew from LA to San Francisco, rented a car, drove to Vineland to see Kevin, couldn't get in, and bailed, just like that?"

"It was Stern's idea. He said he thought they'd let us see him if we went back with some kind of legal document."

"Where'd you guys go after you left Vineland?"

"Drove back to SFO, hopped on a plane and flew back to L.A."

"Stern, too?"

"He was on the same flight back to LA as I was," Roger said. "Swear to God. We sat next to each other the whole way."

"You got a number for him?"

"I'll send you his contact ."

"One last question," I said.

"Sure."

"Why Lester Corbin. Why'd you contact Corbin?"

"Stern's idea. Said I should probably let him know we were gonna be recording the songs."

I thanked him and hung up, telling him how important it was that he be easy to get hold of in the next few days. He said he would be.

Lester Corbin called an hour later. He'd just seen the photo of Roger and the mystery man. He thought I ought to know right away. The man with Roger was Howard Silva.

"Are you sure?"

"I haven't seen him in close to thirty years, but that's him. I'd know him anywhere."

— 20 —

Howard Silva. Band promoter and meter reader. And Vineland visitor, Peter Stern, music producer. And trespasser and murder attempter?

I decided to call Mrs. Sands in Arizona just to corroborate Corbin's identification. She answered on the first ring.

"Oh, Mr. McMahon, I was going to call you today . . . Just a second. I need to let Ella in."

I heard a door open. "Come on in, sweetie," she said, then got back on. "Sorry, but it's already dreadfully hot out, and Ella doesn't do well in the heat."

"I understand," I said, looking at Luther lying out on the deck, his huge head resting on the door's threshold, his tongue hanging out of the side of his mouth.

"I got the picture and your note. I'd have hardly recognized Roger, it's been so long since I've seen him, and he's really grown up."

"I'm sorry about the quality of the photo," I said, trying to keep her talking.

"But you wanted to know if I knew who the older gentleman was, didn't you?"

"Yes, if you recognize him."

"Well," she said firmly. "I recognize him all right. Even though it's been thirty years since I've seen him."

"Howard Silva?" I couldn't help myself.

"Oh, you already knew?"

"I sent the same photo to Lester Corbin and he just called."

"I have just very vague memories of him. He was always in the background, even though he handled all the business stuff."

I wanted to ask her about Johnny, even to tell her what I was thinking, about Ted Knowlton, Sal Black, and what seemed to be hidden messages in Johnny's songs, but it didn't seem appropriate. Not yet anyway. And probably not over the phone.

She thanked me for calling and told me not to hesitate calling anytime.

"Thank you," I said. "I'll probably take you up on that."

It was a gorgeous day, and I had quite a bit of it ahead of me. Alone.

I hoped Becka was enjoying herself at Tahoe.

I went into the kitchen, slopped a turkey sandwich together, and threw it in a little cooler with a couple of Sierra Nevada Pale Ales and a rack of ice cubes. Then I backed Portia out of the garage and headed for Bolinas.

On the way, I stopped in downtown Mill Valley and checked out the box scores while I drank a cup of coffee. It was hard to concentrate with all the bicycle cleats clicking on the sidewalk and the 24-year-olds in butt-padded brightly branded

Lycra shorts talking about their retirement portfolios, so I poured my coffee into a paper cup and got back in the car and headed over the hill to the beach, using my handy-dandy, old-school between-the-thighs cupholder to keep it from spilling.

I got there just before 2:00, parked near the tennis courts, grabbed my cooler, and walked down the street toward the water. Just before I got to where the road dead-ended into the beach, I crossed over to the left side and looked over the fence into the yard of the house closest to the water. Still there, Grace Slick's amazing mosaic swimming pool, empty now, purple, blue, green, and white tiles—some broken away from the gunite and scattered in the foot of green water in the deep end—swirling into a kaleidoscope of colors and memory. I thought back to thirty years earlier. The beach, now cold and deserted, was once alive with sun-drenched naked hippies passing joints, running into the waves, and making love behind rocks, bandana-necked dogs chasing Frisbees, and impromptu guitar jams. I looked up on the hill at the house where hippie writer Richard Brautigan had been found back in 1984, dead some three weeks.

I walked down onto the sand, sat and pulled off my shoes and socks, then stepped into the cold foamy water and let it wash up around my ankles. I walked for a couple of hundred yards, almost to the point, then turned in toward the base of a cliff. I set my cooler down, cracked open a beer, and took a long pull as I watched a handful of fishing boats a couple of miles off shore.

Three things: 1) I needed to figure out the Becka thing. Why was it that I got nervous if we spent too much time together, but once she was gone, and especially now that she was gone with goddamn Lawrence Lundford, she was about all I could think about? Not exactly an original problem, I admit. 2) Of course, Johnny Sands and Jim Rooney, and now Ted Knowlton. And 3) I really wanted to start playing more music again.

Jim Rooney. Christ. I'd have given anything for a copy of that book. Had he written about Johnny Sands' being gay? About Roger being Kevin's son, not Johnny's? And what else did he know and write about? And how did Howard Silva, or Peter Stern, if that's what he was calling himself, fit into it? Had Howard Silva tried to kill Kevin Sands at Vineland? If so, why?

I needed to talk to someone at Narwhal Books. Surely they had something. A sample chapter? Synopsis? Outline? There might have even been something revealing in his original pitch.

I lay down on the sand. It was warm from the sun, and there was very little breeze.

I'm in the back seat of a small airplane flying along the California coast. Out the window below I can see the rocky shoreline and lots of familiar landmarks. Tomales Bay, Point Reyes, the Golden Gate Bridge, Monterey Bay. Then suddenly laughter above the roar of the engine. The pilot. He's wearing headphones and a hat and with his back turned I can't see who it is. A hand on my knee. Becka's. I turn to look at her and it's Sarah Rooney. She smiles and says something I can't understand, then points to the pilot. I try to ask Sarah who's flying the plane, but nothing comes out of my mouth. The pilot adjusts his headphones and reaches down to the instrument panel. It's a guitar amplifier. A hand grabs his wrist, yanks it away from the controls. The pilot struggles to reach the knob, the other hand slams his against the panel.

We're going down. Sarah screams. The pilot turns. It's Johnny. There's a look of sheer terror in his eyes. His passenger laughs, lights a pipe, it flames high, and he tries to pass it to Johnny. Johnny pushes his hand away, yanks back on the steering wheel. It comes off in his hands.

We're on fire Sarah's nails dig into my arms I turn to her and she grabs me hugs me it's Becka kissing me as we plummet making love the passenger takes the steering wheel from Johnny tosses it out the window laughs as it sails off alongside us suddenly turns his hair on fire Silva reaches for Johnny lays a hand gently on his cheek hugs him snaps a guitar string hard on his neck Johnny's head goes limp blood drips from his mouth Sarah screams the waves crash against the rocks the plane flaming Silva laughing heat fire sky.

I woke up in a cold sweat, sat up. It took me a minute to get my bearings. The tide had come in. I looked at my watch. It was nearly two hours later.

I tossed my empties into my cooler, unwrapped my turkey sandwich, and ate it in three bites as I hurried back to my car. I drove over the mountain much faster than I should have.

Instead of going straight home, I hopped on 101 North and headed up to the Marin County Library, in the same blue-domed Frank Lloyd Wright-designed building as Harper's office, and read the July 18, 1976 *Chronicle* story about the plane crash that killed Johnny Sands.

There was nothing in the piece or in any of the follow-up stories to suggest foul play. Johnny had simply gotten on the plane after the gig in Albuquerque, apparently on his way to Denver to catch a commercial flight back to Raleigh, and the plane had gone down against the side of the Sandia Mountains at 10:30 pm. Both he and the pilot were dead when rescuers arrived about a half hour after the crash.

The pilot, Hector Sanchez, a native of Albuquerque, had learned to fly during the Korean conflict and had flown over two dozen reconnaissance missions in 1952 and '53. He had over 1,200 hours experience and was a certified flight instructor himself, one of the most respected in the state, and in fact had been the governor's main charter pilot. Witnesses said it appeared as though he was trying to return to the airport in Albuquerque. The charter company had sold the plane to a salvage company in Las Cruces.

Not very helpful.

When I got home I Googled "plane crash July 16, 1976." First hit: Embry-Riddle Aeronautical University's Hunt Library website, with the National Transportation Safety Board's "Aircraft Accident Reports," listed by year, 1967 to 2020. I clicked on "1976."

There it was, a digitized photograph copy of the 35-page NTSB accident report, with a paragraph-long "Synopsis" of the crash and a detailed table of contents that included "History of the Flight," "Injuries to Persons," and "Damage to Aircraft," as well as "Conclusions," "Findings," "Probable Cause," and "Recommendations."

I started with the synopsis:

At 2230 m.d.t. a Cessna model 411A, N100KR, crashed near Albuquerque, New Mexico. The aircraft was en route to Denver, Colorado. Before the crash, the pilot had requested air-traffic control's permission to return to Albuquerque. There was no further communication from the pilot. The aircraft was destroyed, and the two occupants were killed.

I scrolled to 2.2 (b), "Probable Cause," on page 25. "The National Transportation Safety Board determines that the probable cause of the accident was a collision with terrain."

Well, no, that wasn't the *cause* of the "accident." That *was* the accident.

Your tax dollars at work.

I read on. "Contributing to the accident were the pilot's failure to appreciate the severity of the weather and his failure to take initiative to divert flight before options were reduced."

I scrolled to "Recommendations": "The Safety Board recommends that pilots and controllers study the circumstances of this accident and decide how they could have responded to the conditions involved in this flight in a way that would have prevented the accident."

Thirty-five pages. I didn't have a whole lot, but I did have "no further communication from the pilot."

— 21 —

Becka had her weekly gal-pal happy hour the next day, so I assumed that she'd be back by now. I hated thinking about her and Lawrence Lundford together. It hurt, and made my stomach feel queasy. Her and anyone, actually.

One Sunday morning, not too long after we got together, we drove over to Golden Gate Park in Portia. Becka had wanted to see a Picasso exhibit at the de Young Museum. It was a stunning day. As we drove down Waldo Grade toward the bridge, the water sparkled, glinting silvery and dotted with hundreds of sailboats. On the bridge walkway, cyclists slalomed around skinny joggers gripping water bottles and groups of tourists posing for photos and taking selfies. After checking out the museum—Becka loves the Blue Period—we walked over to the Academy of Sciences and watched the alligators, one of which actually moved an inch once, then drove west through the park to Ocean Beach, then back to Marin. At Stinson Beach, we sat in the car watching the waves and surfers, and then got out and walked down to the water. Becka took off her shoes, hiked up her skirt and walked out into the water up to her knees, then turned to face me, and motioned for me to join her. There was a delicious promise in her gesture, but one I saw no way of being fulfilled immediately. She smiled, looked around, and raised her skirt a little higher, teasingly. I laughed, tossed my shoes up on the beach, and ran into the water with her, my jeans wet up past my knee. Then she grabbed me by the belt, pulled me close to her, and gave me the wettest, sloppiest, most wonderful kiss. "Want to go for a hike in the woods?" she said, pulling away and looking over toward the dunes at the west end of the park.

Afterward, as we lay beneath a blanket I always kept in Portia's trunk for special occasions, we heard a whimpering coming from somewhere nearby.

Becka sat up, the blanket pulled around her, and cocked her head, listening closely. "I think it's coming from over there," she said. Then she scooted back under the blanket, straightened her skirt, pulled on her sweater, stood up, and walked toward some dune grass at the base of a Montery pine. She poked around a bit, then dropped to her knees and reached down. "Oh, my God, Michael," she said, pulling something into her chest. She stood, turned, and came back over to where I was lying. "Look at her, she can't be more than six weeks old."

In her arms she held a tiny black and white dog, maybe part Lab, its nose scrunched up and its ears flapping forward. She sat down beside me, held it in her lap, and pulled the blanket up around its neck. I reached down and ran my hand back over the pup's forehead and down over its ears. "She's shivering," I said.

"She's *freezing*. Come on, let's get her to the car and turn the heat on."

We stood, gathered up the blanket, wrapped the puppy, walked back to Portia. Becka got in and I set the pup on her lap. Then I started the engine and cranked the heater up to high.

"What do you want to do with her?" I said, petting her neck.

Becka shook her head and rubbed the puppy under the blanket. "I don't know," she said. "But we couldn't leave her out there. She'd have died of cold."

"She seems to be warming up a bit," I said.

"Paloma," she said.

"Paloma?"

"Doesn't she look like a Paloma?"

Of course, Picasso's wife's name

She pulled Paloma up from the blanket and held her in front of her so they were face to face, eyes about six inches apart. "Look at that little face."

"What should we do with her?"

"Well, I doubt someone's looking for her. She didn't wander over there. She was dumped." Becka stroked her little forehead. "Poor girl."

"Back to my place?"

"What'll the big guy do?"

"You kiddin'?" I said. "The gentle giant?"

"But he could kill her just playing. Squash her."

"Nah, his instincts are better than that. Besides, we can make a little bed for her, in a box or something."

I put Portia in gear, and we pulled out of the parking lot and drove back over the hill to Mill Valley. When we got back to my place, we turned an old wine-case box on its side with a towel for padding, set it in the bathroom, and pushed Paloma inside. She sat, stared at us for a moment, then turned in two or three circles, lay down, and fell asleep. Luther took one sniff of the pup, then turned and went back by the door and lay down himself. Paloma slept without a peep all night. In the morning, Becka held her on her lap while we drank coffee and read the *Chronicle* and Luther eyed me from across the room.

Although it was difficult, we both admitted that neither of

us could keep Paloma, so that afternoon, we took her to the Marin Humane Society. They promised they'd find her a good home.

— 22 —

I woke up Friday morning and shot Becka a quick email welcoming her home, then decided to try to talk to Kevin again. Spencer had said that sometimes Kevin could remember the tiniest of details. I hoped I'd catch him at one of those times. Tiny details about the night of the plane crash might be wonderfully useful. I called Spencer. He said Kevin was doing well and that I could come up again any time.

"This afternoon?"

"Sure. One-ish?"

"See you then."

I logged onto my computer and Googled Marin County flight schools. There were three, but the most promising looked like AeroInstruction Marin, operating out of Gnoss Field in Novato.

I dialed the "Contact Us" number on their website.

"AeroInstruction Marin, this is Diana. How may I direct your call?"

I identified myself and asked it if were possible to speak to a flight instructor.

There was a brief pause, then, "This is Mark Cramer. I'm an instructor. How can I help you?"

I gave him a bare-bones summary of the Jimmy Rooney

case, including the crash that killed Johnny Sands—Cramer said he loved those old songs and that the crash came up in conversation with the instructors from time to time. I also told him about the accident report indicating that the last communication from the pilot was his request for permission to return to the airport. Cramer said he'd be happy to help in any way that he could.

I got straight to the point. "Is it possible that someone could sabotage a plane so that it would crash a half hour into its flight?"

I could hear him take a deep breath.

"Wow," he said. "Next to impossible. The pre-flight safety checks are so thorough that the pilot would identify any issues. Plus, even back then, before TSA, there was security at airports."

"Even small, local ones?"

"Hmmm . . . well some smaller, uncontrolled airports weren't as secure as others but your sabotager would have to have snuck in in the middle of the night to get access. Plus they'd need to know their way around small planes." He paused again. "I guess there's one way they could do it so that the plane would still pass pre-flight . . . Let's see, they remove the spinner—that's the pointed fairing at the nose of the plane covering the prop hub. Then they could remove five of the six bolts that attach the propeller to the engine. Then they replace the spinner, and *voila*, the plane passes preflight. But once it's in the air, the prop starts to vibrate like crazy and breaks off. The plane's toast."

I was getting hopeful. "Wow, do you think something like that could have happened with Johnny Sands?"

"Not a chance," Cramer said.

"Not a chance?"

"First, they'd never have lasted a half hour in the air. Might not have even gotten off the runway. Also, it woulda been all over that accident report—those guys know what they're doing. And *then*," he went on, "if there *had* been evidence that the plane had been tampered with, there would have been a full-on criminal investigation."

"What if there was a cover-up? The original accident report was bogus?"

"Nah," he said, "There'd have to have been a whole army of guys involved. There's just too much cross-checking and over-sight."

"Shoot, " I said. "Thought I might have been on to some-thing."

"Sorry," Cramer said. "Wish I could be more help."

I thanked him for his time, and he told me not to hesitate if I had any more questions—or wanted to go up with him some time.

I had an hour or so before I needed to head up to Vine-land, so I took Luther for a little stroll around the neighborhood, thanking the lord for iPhones and earbuds and that the Giants were beating the Padres.

When I got home, I nuked a couple of frozen green-chile tamales and washed them down with a Pale Ale, then backed Portia out of the garage, and headed back up to Vineland.

It was a gorgeous day, the sun glinting off the Richardson Bay high tide, the hills of Marin still green, Mt. Tamalpais tow-ering in my rear-view mirror. I thought about stopping at Sono-ma Raceway to see if they were open for a few laps but I'd told

Spencer one-ish. I sped on by, wondering how best to talk to Kevin about the crash, especially since it could have been at least partially responsible for triggering his schizophrenia.

Gretchen was alone at a computer behind the counter when I walked into the lobby. She looked up, smiled, and reached for the ledger book.

"Mr. McMahon," she said. "Dr. Spencer said to expect you."

I signed in and she led me to Spencer's office, the door of which was open. He was sitting at his desk and stood as I walked in. Gretchen walked back down the hall to the lobby.

"Glad you could make it," he said, reaching out to shake my hand. "Kevin's doing surprisingly well. I think he'll be fine with a visitor, although you probably ought to keep it on the short side."

"Sure," I said. "Anything I need to know? I was hoping to ask him about the night of Johnny's crash."

"I don't think so. Come on. We'll just play it by ear. So to speak." He smiled. "See how he does with it."

He led me down the hall and back out onto the common area where Kevin had been sitting before. He was on the same bench, with his guitar, this time singing softly. "Pancho and Lefty."

He looked up as we approached, stopped singing, then playing, but let the last trebly guitar notes sustain.

"Kevin," Spencer said, "you remember Mr. McMahon."

Kevin stood and we shook hands. "Definitely."

Already I could tell he was doing way better.

"Do you mind if he asks you a few questions?"

He shrugged. "Not at all." He sat back down, leaning his guitar beside him against the bench.

Spencer looked at his watch. "I've got some work to do. I'll leave you two for a bit." He gave me the go-easy-on-him look.

I nodded, and he turned and headed back to his office.

I sat down at the other end of the bench.

"Thanks for taking the time to talk to me," I said.

"Sure, man." He pulled a pack of cigarettes out of his front shirt pocket, tapped one out and lit it.

"You doin' okay? I heard about the other night."

He shrugged. "That was some crazy-ass shit."

"I guess."

"Yeah, doing okay."

"Cool to talk a bit more about Johnny?"

"Totally."

I wanted to ease in slowly, not get right to the night of the crash. "Your whole family was really musical, right."

"Yeah, people were always telling us what an amazing fiddle player Dad was. I barely remember."

"Your mom, too."

"Uh huh. Keys, er, organ, and sang like an angel."

"You guys started really young."

"We had a little group with our sister like in high school, until Johnny and I started to get more serious. "

"The Johnny Sands Band."

"Yeah, I was just as serious, but Johnny was the real deal. Wrote great songs, sang great, and the chicks totally dug him."

"Hard on you?"

"Nah, I kinda liked being in the background."

"Must've been hard when he died."

He nodded. "I was a mess." He smiled. "*Was?*"

"I understand."

"Maybe." He reached for his guitar, strummed a G, hammering down on the B on the A string. He took a breath.

"Kevin," I said. "I know about Roger."

He sat back suddenly.

"My nephew?"

"I mean I know the story. I've talked with his mom. Must be hard," I said. "Not seeing your . . . son."

He took a deep breath, shook his head, then seemed to look at something far away. He came back to the moment. "You talked with Carla?"

"Just a couple of days ago. She'd flown up to see you but they wouldn't let her visit the day after you had your late-night . . . encounter."

"No shit," he said again, shaking his head. "He still trying to be a movie star?"

"Or rock and roll star. Or famous screenwriter."

"It *is* hard," he said. "Really hard sometimes. I try not to think about it."

"How long's it been?"

"Carla used to bring him with her when she'd come up, but it's been, Jees, twenty years . . . "

"Sorry."

"It's okay."

I took a deep breath. I couldn't tell him that his son had just been at Vineland.

"Speaking of Roger," he said, "here's something. Remember I told you about how our manager freaked out when Johnny said he was taking my place on the flight back to Raleigh?"

"Right."

"Which was weird. He was a pretty low-key guy. Intense in some ways, but not known for flying off the handle."

"More for keeping the trains running on time," I hear.

"Exactly."

"But we got into it one other time, after a show just about a week before. I'd told him that I wanted to come clean about Roger. My brother and I had talked about it. We were both tired of fakin' it, you know? Our fans thinking Johnny had a kid. Believe me, Johnny would *never* have had a kid."

"Kevin, did your brother say why he wanted to go in your place the night of the crash?"

Kevin shook his head. "No, but I think I know. I think he wanted to tell Mom about him and Teddy. He was going to come out to her, as they say, then tell the world. Sorry," he said again.

"No, it's okay," I said. "I was hoping you'd be comfortable talking about that night."

"I don't know about comfortable, but I can." He buried his face in the palms of his hands.

"You all right?" I said.

He took an intentional breath, like he'd learned it in some class or workshop. "Yeah, I'm fine."

Definitely awkward. I was relieved to see Spencer approaching. "Gentlemen," he said. "How we doin'?"

"We're doin'," I said.

"I'm thinking maybe this is good enough," Spencer said, looking at his watch. "Mr. McMahon?"

I was grateful for his suggestion. "I really should be going anyway."

Kevin reached for his guitar, strummed a couple of chords, then sang from Cat Stevens' "Father and Son":

I was once like you are now, and I know that it's not easy, to be calm when you've found something going on.

We both stood, shock hands. "Thanks for taking the time to talk," I said.

"Sure." He sat back down, and I turned to head back to Spencer's office, Kevin singing, "Take your time, think a lot, think of everything you've got . . . " I had just about reached the automatic doors when the music stopped and Kevin called out, "Hey, McMahon." I turned to see him still sitting on the bench. "Come on back any time."

I smiled and waved, indicating that I would. He gave me a thumbs-up.

— 23 —

Luther woke me up early the next morning, his cold nose on the back of my hand hanging over the side of the bed. I fed him, made a pot of coffee, drank a tall glass of orange juice, toasted a bagel, and headed out the door for the gym. I needed some exercise, and to clear my head.

There were three-on-three games at both ends of the court, Stan Harper and Brian Wolfe totally engrossed in one. I grabbed a ball off the floor against the wall and shot a bit waiting my turn with a couple of other guys. Harper and Wolfe's team won, so the three of us took them on.

Once again, Harper was hot, but Wolfe knew his way around a hoops court himself, and they beat us pretty good. No one was waiting to play, so we ran it back. We beat them in the second game, so played a rubber match, their team winning when Harper popped a three from the top of the key.

"You guys got time for a steam?" Harper asked me, wiping his forehead with a towel.

"Saturday morning," I said. "I got nothin' but time."

"Brian?"

"I gotta spend a few hours in the office this morning getting caught up, but sure," Wolfe said.

We single-filed down the hall to the locker room. I was the first one in the steam room and sat down on my towel. Harper and Wolfe came in a few minutes later, their towels wrapped around their waists. The diffuser hissed, shooting a hot cloud of steam across the floor by our feet. "Yeow, that's friggin' hot," I said, pulling up my knees.

"No shit," Wolfe said.

"Supposed to be," Harper said, then took a pull on his water bottle. Then to me, "What's going on with the Jim Rooney case? Here, want some water?"

I took the bottle and squirted a swallow into my mouth. "Pretty interesting." I didn't want to get to into it then and there.

On a lark I turned to Wolfe. "Stan says you're a cardiologist."

"Uh huh," Wolfe said. "Fifteen years now."

"I got a question," I said. "Hypothetical. Let's say there's this private detective working on a case. His client's wife's husband dies in a car crash, which was supposedly because he went into cardiac arrest and lost control. But this private detective's client thinks her husband might have been murdered, that it wasn't really cardiac arrest."

"That he was run off the road?" Harper said, smirking.

"Of course the private detective, strictly hypothetically, is skeptical, but then a bunch of weird shit happens and this private detective starts to wonder if maybe it was murder after all . . . "

"Strictly hypothetical," Wolfe said.

"Strictly," I said. "So, hypothetically, *strictly* hypothetically, can they be *wrong*? They call it cardiac arrest and it wasn't?"

"I thought that's where you were going. No autopsy, I assume."

"Right."

"How old was he?"

"Sixty-five."

Harper laughed. "Strictly hypothetical."

Wolfe took a deep breath, coughed on the steam. "It's just so hard to know without an autopsy. Usually, they rely on the patient's medical history, and his family's."

"That's the thing," I said. "He'd been treated for A-fib and acute heart failure. And it's what killed his dad."

"Seems like a pretty logical conclusion then. Especially if you don't have a reason to suspect otherwise. Autopsy would have confirmed it."

I nodded. "Okay," I said. "Here's a question. Let's say, hypothetically, that someone did want him dead. Can cardiac arrest be, well, induced?"

He shook his head. "Unlikely," he said. "There've been some studies that show that certain medications can lead to heart failure, but you'd have be taking them for a long time. Non-steroidal anti-inflammatories. Some diabetes and blood pressure meds. But it's not like you could slip one in someone's drink to trigger cardiac arrest."

"Slippin' mickies?" Harper said. "Just like cutting brake cables. I told you, only happens in the movies and on TV."

"I mean if both he and his dad had cardiac issues . . . it just kind of follows," Wolfe said. "Although nothing surprises me anymore."

— 24 —

I slept in Sunday morning, then walked downtown to the Mill Valley Sweetbread Café for a plate of their famous *carnitas* breakfast tacos and a bloody *Maria*. After most of the Sunday *Chronicle* and a leisurely brunch, including a second bloody, I walked home, trying to figure out what the link might be between the plane crash that killed Johnny Sands and the car crash that killed Jim Rooney.

Luther greeted me at the gate, and I loaded him into my pick-up and headed out to the coast, listening to *St. Dominic's Preview,* Van Morrison's second CD, after *Tupelo Honey*, from his early '70s Marin County days.

Meanwhile back in San Francisco
We're trying to make this whole thing blend.

Highway 1, technically California State Route 1, or, in honor of our veterans, Blue Star Memorial Highway, traces the Pacific coast from the tiny northern Mendocino County town of Legget down through Sonoma and Marin counties, across the Golden Gate Bridge, along the western edge of San Francisco, through Santa Cruz, Monterey, Big Sur, and Santa Barbara, on through Ventura, Los Angeles, and Orange counties, finally terminating in Dana Point at its junction with Interstate 5—or, as they say in southern California, "*the* Five."

During the late 1960s and early '70s, it was known as the Hippie Highway, especially its northern stretch—tie-dyed, bandana-ed, longhairs in granny glasses motoring along in brightly hand-painted, peace-signed VW busses stopping for embroidered and bellbottomed brothers and sisters huddled hitchhiking on the roadway shoulder with their "Anywhere" signs and their dogs, an occasional wolf cross but generally of uncertain pedigree.

I knew the road well, at least the 50-mile Marin County stretch, from Muir Beach up to Bodega just over the Sonoma County border. In junior high as a kid on my blue Schwinn Varsity, in high school on my Honda Super Sport, and at least twice a week in the 30 years since, full-throttling in Portia or lumbering along in my pick-up with Luther.

I took Panoramic Highway up out of Mill Valley, winding over and along the southern flank of Mt. Tamalpais, then dropped down to Highway 1 at Muir Beach and followed the highway north.

I pulled over into a dirt turn-out about 20 yards south of where Rooney's Mustang had left the road, a 90-degree bend that forced southbound drivers to make a sharp left away from the cliff. A red-reflectored guardrail blocking about 80% of the turn. I could see where his car had just missed the rail and gone over. And in a vintage Mustang convertible—primitive lap seatbelts, no airbags—he would have been a goner, even if it was only a 20-or-so-foot drop down to the rocks.

I parked, got out, and walked along the roadway toward the bend, the foamy, kelpy waves crashing onto the rocks below. I wondered where Pedro Rodriguez had seen the accident from.

A couple of bearded old fat guys on chopped Harleys *Easy Rider*-ed past, heading north, "Live Free or Die" stitched on the backs of their black leather vests flapping against their white XXL t-shirts, the guy trailing wearing a helmet painted to look like a skull.

When I got to the guardrail I stepped behind it and walked alongside, looking down at the rocks, then sat down on it, my back to the road and the green rolling hills of west Marin, and looked out over the water. A couple of hundred yards out, two spoofs of mist shot up out of the water and dissipated into the air. Gray whales. Probably a mother and her young calf, recently born off the coast of Baja, heading to their summer feeding grounds in Alaska's Bering Sea.

I was a lucky man. This was one of the most gorgeous spots on the planet, and it was basically my back yard. I took a deep breath of wet, salty air and looked over to the spot where Rooney's car had missed the guardrail and where there was a path going down to the rocks below.

Path?

Rodriguez had seen someone get out of his car, scramble over the side of the cliff, climb back up and drive away.

Rooney had been on his way to mail a hard copy of his

book about the Johnny Sands Band to his publisher, but it wasn't among his "personal effects" that the cops had returned to Sarah Rooney.

Rodriguez had seen someone get out of his car, scramble over the side of the cliff, climb back up and drive away.

Holy shit. With the manuscript.

I hustled back to my pick-up, apologized to Luther for not stopping for a swim, cranked a U-ie, and headed back over the hill to Mill Valley.

— 25 —

When I got home I poured myself a Mt. Tam Pale Ale, sat down in front of my computer, and typed "Narwhal Books" into Google's search box. Ads, lists of books they'd published, reviews. I clicked on their home page link, then "Contact Us," which had several links underneath. I clicked on "Submissions."

We are currently accepting new manuscripts in the following genres: memoir, biography, food and wine, and finance. To submit a book proposal, please use the form below to submit a cover letter describing your project in a paragraph or two, as well as your qualifications, including connections to your topic and your publishing history; a four-to-six page summary of your book; a table of contents; and a sample chapter. Please include your payment of $100. We generally respond to proposals within six months.

Below was a box for each of the requirements, as well a form for the requisite credit-card payment information.

So unless Jim Rooney's book proposal had been deleted—which seemed unlikely after only three months—it must have still been on file at Narwhal Books.

I went back to the "Contact Us" page and clicked on "Editorial Offices," where there was the general email address and an 800 number, as well as their hours: Weekdays only. I'd have to wait till tomorrow to call.

I thought about Salvador Black, the companion listed in Ted Knowlton's obituary as one of his survivors. Hugely common last name of course, but Salvador? Not so much. Long shot, but what the hell. Google Visit Number Two of the day.

Bingo!

Three hits.

And I could rule out two immediately. The first, a 45-year-year-old teachers'-union leader from Miami, the second, an 80-year-old retired precinct judge from Webb County, Texas, "married to his beloved wife, Connie, for 55 years."

And then there was the 70-year-old children's-book illustrator from San Francisco who, according to his publisher's bio, had been "one of the founders of the City's pioneering AIDS Partners Support Group."

Unfortunately, there was no contact information.

Ordinarily, I'm not much of Facebook fan, but I do have an account and a few "friends."

I went to my page and typed Salvador Black into the Search box.

There were four listed, but only one from San Francisco. I

sent him a friend request. I got a response almost immediately: "Say Hello to your new friend Salvador Black." I didn't say hello but went to his page and his profile photo. He looked a bit like Ricky Ricardo.

I sent him a short private message identifying myself, very briefly describing the case and the connection to Ted Knowlton, and asking if he would be interested in talking, either in person or on the Facebook "platform."

He wrote back:

I read about Jim Rooney's death in the Chronicle, I didn't know him, but Teddy used to talk about the old days with Johnny Sands, I'd be happy to talk tho I don't know if I'd be much help.

He included a phone number and an email address.

Salvador Black. Happy to talk.

Did I already say "Bingo"?

Suddenly, I had two new avenues to explore. I called Black and made a lunch date for the next day. He lived in North Beach, so we decided to meet at Original Joe's, the historic Italian restaurant that had relocated from the Tenderloin after being destroyed by fire in 2007. Always packed and loud. Shouting waiters in tuxes. Red table wine in water glasses. Puffy red Naugahyde benches at the booths. San Francisco writers and artists and drinkers eating seafood pasta lunches at the counter.

Perfect. I needed my Original Joe's fix.

He said he'd meet me at the bar.

Even better.

— 26 —

I woke up shortly after 8:00 and took Luther for a walk. A beautiful, classic south-Marin spring morning, just a crisp hint of dampness from the Bay hanging in the air.

At 9:00 sharp I called Narwhal Books.

Of course I was instructed to listen carefully to the entire recording "as our menu has recently changed" and I didn't know the extension of "the person I wish(ed) to speak with."

Instead, I hit 0 and got Heather, who connected me with Don Peterson in editorial.

I explained why I was calling and asked if there were any possibility that they might still have Rooney's submission material and if so was there any way that I could see it.

He was hesitant, naturally. "We don't see this every day but coincidentally someone else contacted me a few weeks ago requesting the same information. I just need to contact our legal department to get the form. Let me get back to you."

I told him that I understood but emphasized how important the information could turn out to be.

He called back an hour later. He'd just emailed me the form.

I downloaded it, filled it out and sent it back.

He wrote back that he would be able to send PDFs of the cover letter, the summary, the table of contents, and the sample chapter the next day.

I was looking forward to my meeting with Salvador Black almost as much I was looking forward to the lunch and water glasses at Original Joe's.

It was too early to head over to the City, though, so I grabbed my gym bag and stopped at the club on my way. Did a half hour on the treadmill, fifteen minutes on the rowing machine, and twenty minutes of free weights, then a quick steam.

It was 11:30 when I was walking out to the parking lot. Perfect timing, thank you very much.

Parking in North Beach can be a pain, but I got lucky and found a spot on Columbus, almost right in front of City Lights Bookstore—just a short walk down the street and then a half block up Union to Original Joe's.

Black was already at the bar when I got there, sitting on a stool at the far corner. Lucy nowhere in sight.

I caught his eye and waved. He indicated the stool next to him. I walked over, we shook hands, and I squeezed in next to him.

"Thanks for taking the time to meet with me," I said.

He took a sip from his water glass and shrugged. "Not like I've got much else to do these days. Glass of wine?"

"Of course," I said.

He waved at the balding, 60-ish, white-aproned bartender, called out "Guido," and held up two fingers. Guido showed up with another water glass and a half-full decanter of red wine, filled mine close to the top and refilled Black's.

We chatted for a bit about North Beach—turned out he'd lived in the neighborhood for nearly 40 years—and City Lights and the different bars and how much the City had changed.

Guido showed up a few minutes later with an order pad. I

went with the linguine pesto with sautéed prawns, and Black ordered the veal piccata. Guido tore the sheet off the pad, turned and set it in a clip on a track on the chrome counter between the bar and the kitchen, then set a napkin-covered basket of sliced sourdough and two water glasses—filled with ice water—in front of us.

I tore off a slice of bread and spread a pad of butter on it.

Black sipped his wine. "Teddy and I hadn't been together very long when he got sick," he said. "But I felt like we had. We both thought that we'd be together for the rest of our lives. I guess that was right in his case."

"Must've been hard," I said.

He nodded. "It was. Friends were dying all around us. We thought it was the end of the world. And after this paradise we'd found."

"But . . ."

"Never got sick," he said. "I actually felt guilty about it."

Guido set our plates in front of us.

"But the band played on," he said.

I nodded.

"You're probably too young to remember, but it was horrific. Good folks dying miserable deaths and people actually saying that it was"—he made finger quotes—"God's way of cleansing the world of fags." He shook his head and smiled ironically. "Doesn't work. Most people don't realize that the two giraffes on Noah's ark were lesbians . . . Good thing one was pregnant."

I laughed. "That one of your children's books?"

His eyebrows shot up. "Now *there's* an idea for a book. *The Giraffe with Two Mommies.*

"Guaranteed best seller," I said, then: "Did Ted . . . Teddy, ever talk about his days with the Johnny Sands Band? Or about Johnny at all?"

Black nodded. "A bit," he said. "I think he didn't want to make a big deal of the fact that his first boyfriend was a rock star." He took a breath. "Sorry."

"No, no. Go on," I said.

"Apparently he and Johnny Sands had known each other since junior high, met in band class. Johnny played trumpet, Teddy played trombone." He laughed. "They got to be pretty good friends in high school—they both loved 1950s movies and musicals, especially *Guys and Dolls* and *Some Like it Hot*." He shook his head. "Oh, and *Rebel Without a Cause*." He laughed softly. "Can I paint more of a stereotype?"

I'd hardly made an *al dente* in my pasta. Black cut into his veal picatta.

"Anyway, Teddy told me that after high school they realized that they loved each other and wanted to be together. Remember, this wasn't only 1973, it was Raleigh, North Carolina. The south. Not exactly San Francisco. Or even Greenwich Village. And this was right when the Johnny Sands Band was beginning to take off. He and Johnny figured the only way for them to be together was for Teddy to be a sort of unofficial roadie. He'd handle all of their equipment on their tours, and travel with them. Who would know?"

"Did anyone?"

"The guys in the band had to have. Or at least suspected. And I think Johnny's brother's girlfriend. And their manager."

"Word is," I said, "that Johnny's brother Kevin was supposed to be on the plane that night and then the two of them got into some kind of argument with Silva, and Johnny ended up getting on the plane."

"Teddy told me that story."

"Any idea what the argument was about?"

"Teddy always wondered," he said, "but he did tell me one thing. Johnny was trying to come out, way back then, but he wanted to tell his mom first. So he took his brother's place at the last minute."

"And Kevin had been planning to fly back to see his girlfriend and kid."

Black took a breath. "Partly," he said, "but Teddy thought that he wanted to talk to his mom, too. That he wanted to tell her about Roger, that he was his son, not Johnny's."

"So both of them wanted to talk to their mom but for different reasons? Or really the same reason . . . "

"Think about it," Black said, "If Kevin told his mom about Roger, and then told their fans, they'd all wonder why the band had passed Johnny off as the dad. And, *if* Johnny came out to his mom and then told his fans, well, remember, it was the mid-'70s."

"Elton John was still down the hall in a closet."

"*Exactly.* And they'd figure out why the band had passed Johnny off as the dad. And they'd feel let down by the lie, and the legions of Johnny Sands-crazy girls would be left without a fantasy. Probably the end of Johnny Sands-mania. That's my theory anyway," Black said, taking a swallow of wine and wiping his upper lip with the starched white napkin.

"So," I said, "if Kevin had been on the plane he wouldn't have gotten home to tell his mom about Roger, and the band could have continued on, with rock star Johnny, to all the world Roger's dad, at the helm."

Black shrugged.

Guido walked down the bar and stopped in front of us. "Anything else, gentlemen? "

Black and I looked at each other and shrugged. "Guess not," I said.

"I think we're good." Black added.

Guido slid the bill onto the bar between our plates, and I grabbed it.

"Thank you," Black said. "That's awfully sweet."

"My pleasure. Thanks again for taking the time to talk."

"*My* pleasure," Black said. "Next time, I buy."

He spun on his stool, stood, reached for his water glass and polished off his wine. We shook hands, and he pulled a tweed Irish flatcap out of his back pants pocket, set it jauntily on his head, then turned and wove his way through the clatter and crowd of customers and waiters, pushed open the front door, and disappeared up Union Street.

That night I had my class. Ordinarily, I'd have spent a day or two preparing, but I'd been so caught up in the Jim Rooney case that I'd barely even thought about it. Fortunately, we were starting group presentations that night. I'd learned my second or third semester that student presentations not only made my job easier but that the students also learned more. Classic win-win.

That night's presentations were on The Band, Robert Johnson, and Bo Diddly. I wrapped things up in the last hour playing YouTube clips with the Big Bopper, Buddy Holly, Richie Valens, Stevie Ray Vaughan, Ricky Nelson, John Denver, and Ronnie Van Zant, Steve and Cassie Gaines from Lynyrd Skynyrd. All killed in plane crashes. Of course, Shelley Martin brought up Patsy Cline. Good call. I let her play a clip. Then I played some more Johnny Sands.

Definitely over on the dark side that night. I felt kind of bad as my students filed out of class, mostly quiet, without their usual yakkety-yak about what bar they were heading to.

I stopped by the department office after class to check my mail. Nothing interesting, as usual—various flyers for campus events and cards from publishers announcing new textbooks. Round-filed them. There was a thick stack of postcards, though, rubber-banded together with a note indicating that instructors were to pass them out to students. I dropped the bundle into my bag, then walked over to the Owl and had a quick Jameson's over before heading home. Exhausted, as I always was after class, I tossed my school bag on the sofa, filled Luther's water bowl, and crawled into bed. Still no word from Becka.

— 27 —

I slept fitfully that night, finally fell hard asleep around 5:00, then woke at 8:30 with a start to a whimper and a cold Newfoundland nose on my arm. I reached over to the nightstand and grabbed my phone, even knowing it was probably too early for Rooney's submission material from Don Peterson at Narwhal Books.

Nothing yet, of course.

I fed Luther and drank a cup of coffee while I read the *Chronicle*. Mick LaSalle, the movie critic, was in fine form, panning a new documentary on the Back Street Boys.

A little after 9:00 I got a ping on my phone. Email from Narwhal.

I sat down in front of my computer and logged on.

Peterson's cover letter was brief. "Please find attached the complete material from Jim Rooney's submission for his book proposal re a memoir from his days as a member of The Johnny Sands Band."

There were four attachments.

I read through the cover letter. Not much of interest. Basically Rooney's saying that he wanted to tell the story of the band's origins through the night of the crash, identifying himself as the drummer of the band, and suggesting that he had some "behind-the-scenes" stories to tell.

The summary of the book went into more detail, of course, but still didn't reveal much more than public knowledge about the band's story, although it did make clear that Rooney had planned to start the book with the night of the crash and then flash back to the boys' meeting in school, follow the band's rise to stardom, and circle back to that night of their final concert. The table of contents confirmed as much: "Chapter 1: The Crash"; "Chapter 2: A Musical Family"; "Chapter 3: Music and Football: Four Kids in High School." And so on, up to the last one: "Chapter 23: 'I Guess It Doesn't Matter Anymore.'"

I opened "Sample Chapter" and read:

Chapter 1: The Crash
Johnny Sands died on July 17, 1976, when his char-
tered plane crashed outside Albuquerque, New Mexi-

*co, following a sold-out concert . He was 23. Already,
his songs had changed the popular music of the 20th
century. One can only wonder what his impact might
have been had he continued to enrich the world with
his songs and stories.*

*One can also wonder why Johnny was even on
the plane, when his brother, guitar player Kevin, had
booked the flight for himself.*

*One can also wonder what would have become of
the Johnny Sands Band if word had gotten out about
who Johnny really was.*

*And one might wonder—as I do—whether the
crash that took Johnny's life that fateful night might not
have been an accident.*

*I was there that night. I played drums for the band
from the beginning. I knew Johnny well. I myself have
wondered—wondered whether I should tell the story.
But it's time. Let me tell you about the Johnny Sands
Band and the night Johnny died.*

"Might not have been an accident . . . "?

Really? Maybe I wasn't crazy after all.

But then Mark Cramer had said that it would be almost impossible to sabotage a plane to induce a crash.

Besides, why would someone want a plane to go down with
one of the members of the most popular band in the country on
board—Kevin *or* Johnny?

I read on. Not much after that teaser. Just sort of an over-
ture, Rooney's setting the stage for the rest of the book by estab-

lishing his credentials as a high school pal of the Sands brothers and a founding member of the band. The chapter ended with a couple of paragraphs about the early days of American country music and Rooney's claim that despite their electric instruments, the Johnny Sands Band was not all that far removed from the Carter Family and Jimmie Rogers and the other artists Ralph Peer recorded in the summer of 1927 in Bristol, Tennessee.

— 28 —

I was just getting ready to head out the door for the market to pick up something for dinner when I noticed that all the crap in my school bag had spilled out onto the sofa when I'd tossed it there the night before. My grade book, a yellow pad, a thin plastic three-ring binder, several CDs, a handful of hard-copy articles I'd clipped from old *Rolling Stones*, and the stack of postcards. I picked the postcards up and read the little note on top more closely:

Please distribute the enclosed cards to your students. Date rape is an increasingly alarming issue, particularly among college students, and they need to be informed as to how to prevent it as well as equipped with a list of resources should they themselves or an acquaintance become victims of this crime. Thank you in advance for working with us to address this problem. Marin Community College Police Department.

I slid one of cards out of the stack. Slick, nicely produced, with an image of the school's logo, the words "College of Marin Founded 1926" in a wheel circling three stylized neo-classical arches, below which was the school's motto: "Par Oneri," Latin for "Equal to the Task."

I turned it over and read the back. They had listed statistics on the frequency of date rape, including a line graph showing its increase over a five-year period, and a bulleted list of guidelines of ways to avoid it, including: Go out in groups, meet first dates in public places, let roommates know when to expect you home, don't accept a drink from a stranger, never leave a drink unattended. There was also a brief paragraph that explained that several "date-rape drugs" exist that are "colorless, odorless and tasteless" and can be slipped into a drink to make a victim "feel physically weak or pass out." And then there was a list of local and national resources, including the 800-number for the National Sexual Assault Telephone Hotline. An italicized, large-fonted line across the bottom read, "Stay Safe This Summer."

I slid the card back into the stack, stuffed everything into my bag, and dropped the stack of cards on top. I would distribute them next Monday night.

I was headed out and literally had my hand on the doorknob when I did a double take: *colorless, odorless and tasteless*, can make a victim feel *physically weak or pass out*.

Holy moly! It would have been next to impossible to sabotage Johnny Sands' chartered plane, but could the pilot have been drugged?

I went back to my computer and Googled "date rape drugs."

This was "Bingo!" upper case.

"BINGO!"

Victims of date rape, or "drug-facilitated sexual assault," I read, have typically been dosed with one of three common drugs. "Rohypnol," known on the street as "roofies," was the most frequently used, its effects—sleepiness, confusion, weakness, and trouble breathing—kicking in after around 30 minutes and lasting several hours. GHB, known for slowing heartbeat and making breathing difficult—and causing death in high doses—took effect in 15 to 30 minutes and lasted three to six hours. Ketamine caused hallucinations, increased heartbeat, raised blood pressure, and made victims feel completely disoriented. Its effects lasted 30 to 60 minutes.

All three were "colorless, odorless, and tasteless," their effects exacerbated by alcohol. All were relatively easy to come by.

Could someone have drugged Hector Sanchez before he and Johnny left Albuquerque for Denver?

I called Corbin in Santa Fe. Did he know anything about Hector Sanchez? And what was his relationship with the band?

Turns out Sanchez was not only one of the most well-respected charter pilots in the Albuquerque area, but he was a huge fan of the Johnny Sands Band. "Sort of a guy groupie," Corbin said. "He was at like half our concerts in the western states."

"That last Albuquerque concert, too, I assume?"

"Definitely. In fact, he got a comp ticket that night since he was going to be flying Kevin up to Denver."

"Kevin gave him the ticket?"

"Oh, no," Corbin said. "We couldn't do that. If we wanted to comp a friend or family member at a concert, we had to go through Silva. He handled all that shit. In fact, I remember seeing them talking back stage."

"Wait," I said. "Sanchez got a comp ticket *and* a back stage pass?"

"I guess," Corbin said. "Silva was always passing out comps, but the back-stage thing was kinda weird. I guess since he was gonna fly Kevin out after the show. Maybe so they could go out the back door. I don't know."

I wondered about the lavish bars and buffets I'd heard about back stage at rock concerts

"Maybe," Corbin said, "but not at our shows. Silva ran a tight ship. There was always a long folding table with bowls of candy bars—Johnny was famous for Nestle's Crunches and Reese's Peanut Butter Cups—but that was it. No alcohol, nothing like that."

"Just soft drinks?" I asked.

"Coke, root beer, 7-Up, that was it. Maybe why we never trashed hotel rooms after shows."

"Or threw televisions off balconies into swimming pools?" I said.

"Welcome to the Hotel California," Corbin sang.

I told Corbin about what I'd been reading about date rape drugs and asked him if he thought Silva could have provided Sanchez with a "soft drink."

"Sure," Corbin said. "Woulda been easy. The guys who got backstage passes usually wandered around totally oblivious. Not that it happened all that often."

I thanked Corbin for his time, told him I'd keep him posted, and hung up.

Stan Harper had told me that brake cables getting cut by bad guys only happens on television and movies. Sorry, Stan. Wednesday morning the brakes went out on Portia, and it wasn't an accident or lack of maintenance on my part.

In fact, it was my master cylinder. Punched. Drained.

The thing is, on television, brakes fail when the driver's out on some mountain road and can't slow down to negotiate a turn, then barrels off a cliff. But that wasn't the case here. Portia's brakes gave out as I backed down the driveway. I couldn't stop as I crossed the street and T-boned the driver's side of my neighbor Raven's blue Prius. Some serious body damage on the door of her little tin cracker box. At least her "Co-exist" and "Vegans Rock" bumper stickers remained unscathed.

I knocked on Raven's door. She answered, barefoot, her denim jeans rolled up to just below her knees, a thin mother-of-pearl necklace dropping down behind her "Make Coffee Not War" sleeveless top. Her beginning-to-gray hair was twirled in a knot on the back of her head. She was holding pruning shears. I explained what happened, apologized, and told her that my insurance would cover costs of repair. She followed me out to the street, covered her mouth with her hand when she saw the dent.

"Brigid," she said softly.

"Brigid?"

"My girl. Named for the Celtic goddess of healing. Now she's going to need some healing herself."

She took a deep breath, thanked me, and headed back inside.

I took a closer look at Portia's right rear fender. It was banged up a bit it but nothing that a few spatulas of Bondo couldn't take care of, though I'd farm out the painting to a pro.

But that would have to wait.

Someone wanted to hurt me. Someone didn't like me messing around with the Jim Rooney-Johnny Sands stuff.

Even if they didn't realize that you can't sabotage the brakes on a car in such a way that they don't fail until some time into an outing.

Except on television.

But I'd have to be more careful for a while.

In fact, I called my pal Denny at the Mill Valley PD and told him about it, and a bit about the case. He said he'd keep an eye on my place.

— 29 —

Originally, I'd planned to fly back down to LA to talk to Roger but decided that maybe I ought to stick a little closer to home. I also wondered whether Roger might be sticking a little closer to home, too.

Mine.

Though he didn't seem like someone who'd try to kill me— especially by making my brakes go out.

Though he did seem like someone with the mechanical wherewithal to botch it if he did.

I called him Thursday morning and tried a new tack. Instead of challenging him, I tried suggesting that I needed his help. Flattery, you know. Besides, I did need his help. I needed to figure out the Howard Silva-Peter Stern-meter-reader thing. Could Roger really not know that Silva and Stern were the same guy? Could he really not know that Kevin was his dad and not his uncle?

I decided not to ask him why he'd never sent me Stern's contact information, like he'd said he would.

He answered right away. "Mr. McMahon." Aha! At least he'd added me as a contact. Talk about flattery.

"Mr. Sands."

"I've been meaning to call you," he said. No wonder he'd never been successful as an actor. I'd never heard anything less believable-sounding.

I let it slide. "Yeah, I meant to get back to you sooner, too. Been doing okay?"

He said that he had.

"Good to hear," I said, trying to sound like an old buddy. Then: "Listen, Roger. I kinda need your help."

"*My* help?"

"Yeah, I'm kinda confused about something." I trailed off.

"Not sure I can help," he said. "But fire away."

"Well," I said. "I've been thinking about your visit with Peter Stern to Vineland to see your uncle . . . "

"Right. We talked about that."

"Roger," I said. "I have it on good authority that your Peter Stern and the Johnny Sands Band's manager Howard Silva are one and the same. The same person."

Silence.

Finally: "Impossible."

I tried to imagine his face. Eyes wide in terror that I knew or a scowl at the preposterousness of my claim?

"Are you fucking kidding me?" he said. "You're trying to tell me that Peter Stern was the band's manager?"

"That's what I'm saying, dude." I thought better than to add: "And also '70s radio programmer R.C. Memphis and a Pacific Gas and Utilities meter reader."

"Come on! Really?"

"Really. Or thus spake Lester Corbin—you know him, I think—and your grandmother. Photo ID-ed from security cam from your visit to Vineland."

"You're not fucking with me?"

"I'm not fucking with you."

"Well, shit. That's just batshit crazy is what this is."

"Look, Roger," I said. "I need to talk to Stern. Or whatever his name is."

I could hear him take a breath. "I get that," he said. "I'll send you his contact info. I promise this time."

I was beginning to believe him. I thanked him and hit End Call. My phone vibrated seconds later.

"Peter Stern." New contact.

Now what? No surprise that the Zombies' "Time of the Season" was stuck in my head: *What's your name? Who's your daddy?* I sang it over and over to myself.

I tapped my new contact.

Hit the highlighted phone number.

Four rings, then the telltale pause that told me it was going to voice mail.

Of course. Probably looked like a robo call to him. Or one from a brilliant private detective about to bust his ass.

"Hello. You've reached the voice mailbox of Peter Stern. Please leave a detailed message at the beep, and I will return your call shortly."

"Hello, Mr. Stern," I said. "My name's Mike McMahon, and I'm actually trying to get a hold of a gentleman named Howard Silva and was told that you might be of some assistance. I'm also hoping that you might be able to refer me to a good auto-body shop and a mechanic that specializes in brakes. Hope to hear from you soon."

I hit End Call.

— 30 —

Actually, I didn't expect to hear from him soon.

Though I thought my little voicemail might spark something.

Apparently, it did.

Friday night, Becka and I met for dinner at Louis Chan's, her suggestion. She was wearing a faded denim skirt to her calves, Birkenstocks, a bone-colored cambric blouse, and dangly silver peace-sign earrings.

We shared the #5 dinner plate—shrimp soup, veggie egg rolls, crab-fried wontons, sweet and sour pork, broccoli chicken, and house chow mein.

I updated her on the Jimmy Rooney case, including the failed brakes, my talk with Roger, and the voicemail I'd left with Stern/Silva. She told me how her semester was winding down—apparently she had some hotshot kid in a creative-writing class who wanted to write detective novels.

She said she thought that he could probably do better. I told her that I thought it was a great idea. Especially if he could come up with a smart, insightful, good-looking, and likeable detective. Who used lots of sentence fragments. Effectively. If sometimes unnecessarily.

The evening was a bit awkward, but I'd missed her so much. Even reading our fortunes seemed forced. Hers was about needing to appreciate the darkness in order to see the stars. Mine was about how valuable it is to learn the ways of other cultures. Oh.

As we were getting ready to leave, my phone buzzed in my pocket. I ignored it. Robo call, probably.

We hugged in the parking lot, and she drove off down Miller Avenue.

Probably heading for Lawrence Lundford's place.

When I got home, my front door was ajar. Fuck. I took a breath and walked in tentatively.

Peter Stern/Howard Silva was sitting in my favorite chair in my living room. He had turned it to face the front door.

A Glock 19 was lying across the left armrest.

Double fuck.

"Mr. McMahon." He picked up the gun, examined it ironically, then pointed it at me like he was aiming out the window of Big 5 Sporting Goods thinking of buying one. "Nice place."

"Thanks."

"You wanna pull the door closed there?" He waved at the front door with the pistol, then set it on his thigh, his hand still resting on it.

I pulled the door shut behind me and pointed to my second-favorite chair. "Mind if I sit down."

"Not at all," he said. "That one's not as comfortable, though." He had more than a slight southern drawl.

I took a breath and walked over and sat down across the

room from him. He put his feet up on the coffee table, crossing his legs at the ankle, and used the heel of his boot to push a *Rolling Stone*, a *New Yorker*, and my homemade cribbage board out of his way. He still had his hand on the pistol on his thigh. Looked pretty fit for a guy in his sixties.

"You should watch some YouTube clips on brake jobs," I said.

He laughed. "Fuck you."

"Seriously. If you'd done it right, we wouldn't be sitting here playing this little game."

"'Little game,'? Mr. McMahon? Or can I call you Mike?"

"Anything you want, just not late for dinner."

"Fucking smart ass."

"Thank you very much. And what do I call you? Mr. Howard Silva? Mr. Peter Stern? M.C. Memphis? Or just asshole? Oh, or Lovely Peter Meter Reader."

"Nice." He shook his head, then lifted the pistol up and aimed it right it at my crotch.

"Look," I said. "I assume the point of your coming calling is to kill me—or at least get me to reconsider my current employment situation."

"Something like that."

"Sorry," I said. "I have a contract with a client. I'm not going to bail on her just because some thug breaks into my house and aims his little pistol at me."

"Asshole." He rotated his arm toward the kitchen and shot through the door out to the back porch. The glass shattered on the floor inside and out. "You don't think I'm serious?"

Surely Raven would have heard the shot. I hoped she'd call

the cops. Not everyone can co-exist.

"Oh, I think you're serious," I said. "Just incompetent. See brake job."

He snorted. "Really? Incompetent? See Johnny Sands and Jim Rooney. See one Pedro Rodriguez."

I licked my forefinger and made three air-scoreboard points for him. "Well done. You must be proud of yourself."

He shrugged. "Hey, a guy's gotta do what a guy's gotta do."

"And assholes gotta do what assholes gotta do."

He licked his finger and gave me a point of my own. "Good one."

"Tell me about Jim Rooney," I said.

He shook his head. "That one scared the shit out of me, but I'm actually kind of proud of it now. I was just following his little Mustang along the coast out there, trying to figure out some kind of plan. I knew he had the book with him. What the fuck, I thought, and just stepped on it and pulled up alongside him. He looked over at me, I waved, he missed the turn. Flew off the fucking cliff."

"Rodriguez?" I said.

"Just covering my bases. Once I knew you were on the case I knew you'd want to track him down."

"Too bad you couldn't make it a nice even four."

"Oh, I plan to," he said.

"I'm talking about Kevin."

He scowled. "Dropped the ball on that one."

"But why try to kill *him* again all these years later?"

He laughed, then rubbed his thumb and forefinger together. "Cash, dude. Thousands just going to waste every month. Our little contract back in the day? Fifty percent of everything to me, the other 50% divided among the four of them."

"Sounds fair," I said.

He laughed. "Those guys were so fucking naïve. I booked their shows, shopped their records around. They loved me. I don't think they even read the contract, which also stipulated that 100% of the royalties from the songs go to the last of the five of us in the event that"—he smirked—"the others shall become deceased."

"So Corbin's on your list, too?"

"Exactamundo."

"But why try to kill Johnny that night? He was the band's bread and butter. Your ticket to, what . . . ?

"As they say, my bad." He looked over the barrel of his pistol at me. "I wanted to kill Kevin—get him out of the way. He was supposed to be on the plane that night, which is why I drugged the pilot. I wanted all their fans to keep thinking that Roger was Johnny's son, not Kevin's. If Kevin went down, I could keep up the façade. That Johnny had a son. But then fucking Kevin decided that he wanted to tell the whole world that Roger was his kid, not Johnny's. Then the assholes switched places and everything fucking fell apart."

"Someone probably heard that shot," I said.

"And Jim Rooney knew everything."

"My hippie neighbor's probably already called the cops."

He shrugged. "Raven? Nice gal. We chatted the other day. You weren't home." He laughed. "Raven's never heard a gun shot. She probably thought it was a tank of patchouli oil exploding. Bummer about her car."

Out of the corner of eye, I caught a glimpse of movement in the kitchen. Luther. He looked at me, then at Silva, then bounded into the living room, snarling like a rabid wolf. He flew straight over the coffee table for Silva, who turned and fired twice into his huge chest, Luther's 150 pounds landing in a limp black mass on Silva's lap.

Silva's gun fell to the floor as he tried to push Luther off of him.

I picked it up and aimed it at his forehead, just as there was a knock at the door.

"Mill Valley PD," a voice said. "It's Denny. Everything okay, Mike?"

"Fine," I said, though it wasn't. My boy was dead. "Come on in."

— 31 —

Sarah Rooney was waiting for me at bar at the Owl Saturday afternoon as I walked in. She was wearing a sleeveless summer dress and suede-strap wedgie sandals. She held a glass with something brown in it. I sat down on the stool next to her. There was already a glass of something brown on the bar in front of me. I took a sip. Jameson's. Of course

"Thanks," I said.

"Thank *you*."

A copy of the LP *Sandy Morning* also lay on the bar, its cardboard sleeve dinged and showing its age. I picked it up and turned it over. Signed, by each of the band members.

"Jimmy would have wanted you to have it," she said.

"Thank you. This means a lot."

"Thanks for the phone call last night."

"Kinda late, sorry, but I figured you'd want to know."

"Oh, yeah. Definitely." She took a sip of her drink. "It seems like you . . . " She hesitated. "Were lucky. You might have . . ."

"Gotten killed?" I said.

"I didn't want to say it."

"Turns out Denny and his pal were on their way over anyway. My security company had called the Mill Valley PD after Silva cut the cable and I didn't return their call. Then they got a report of a gun shot."

She let out a soft whistle.

"Hey, you could be a P.I. yourself with a whistle like that," I said.

"So it is Howard Silva."

"Yep. Bye-oh, Silva."

"Seriously," she said. "You were in—"

"Deep doo-doo?"

"I didn't want to say it."

"I know. I was."

"Crazy," she said.

"Yep."

"So it's all over?"

"Hardly. They arrested him for breaking and entering, but Denny knew what I'd been up to and put the screws to him. Apparently he totally came clean once they got him down to the station. Maybe he thought he'd get off easier that way."

"Will he?"

I shrugged. "I don't know. The trial, or trials, are still a long ways off. Things move slowly in the system."

"Trials? Plural?" Sarah said.

"Most likely. Depends on what the DA wants to pursue. There's no statute of limitations for murder in New Mexico, so they could go after him for Johnny, too. There's a good chance he'd end up with two sentences. And 20 years might be life for a guy his age, even if they let him serve them concurrently."

She nodded. Took a sip of her drink. "I'm still confused about some things," she said. "First of all, what was he doing in your house? What, was he going to kidnap you? Dump you in the bay?"

"I don't know," I said. "I think he was desperate. He knew I was on to him and panicked. He didn't count on Luther."

"Sorry," she said.

I took a breath, fought back a tear. "One of the great ones."

"To Luther," she said. We clinked glasses.

"To Luther."

"So he wanted Jimmy out of the way not only because of the book but because he was afraid his little income stream would dry up? I don't get it. Jimmy hardly got any of those royalties. I think he used his little bit to buy car parts. Not much of an income stream."

"Unless he got Kevin out of the way, too. Those places are $6,000 a month up in the wine country. Plus, once Kevin was dead, the only former band member in line for royalties would have been Lester Corbin."

"He would've been next?"

"He would have been next."

She shook her head softly.

"On top of that, Silva assumed that Jimmy would have written about the night Johnny Sands' plane went down, implicating him. If that got out, he'd at least be a suspect in a murder. Remember, no statute of limitations in New Mexico."

"How'd he think he'd get away with it?"

"I don't know," I said. "But here's a possibility. Roger. He implicates Roger. Roger just wants to record some of the old songs—he thinks Johnny's his dad—so Silva tries to make it look like Roger's trying to get in on the deal."

"Which is why he brought Roger along the first time he went to Vineland?"

"Thank you, Jessica Fletcher," I said.

"I loved that show!"

"Angela Lansbury was wonderful."

"Agreed," she said, then took a sip of her drink. "What about Mr. Meter Reader?" she said. "I don't get that."

"I think Silva just wanted to make sure there were no more hard copies of the book, anywhere. He finds out when you're going to be gone, makes one quick visit, and he's got his bases covered. He already had the computer."

"And what about Roger?"

"I called him this morning. He seemed a bit rattled by it all but said he'd fly up tomorrow. Said he'd see if his mom could come along. Kevin's expecting him. This time."

"Family reunion?"

"Exactly."

"So what are you going to do with yourself for the summer?" she said. "No more students to enlighten. Jimmy Rooney case closed."

I pulled my top lip across my teeth and did my best Bogart. "Not closed, shweetheart," I said.

"That's good."

"Thank you."

"But your part's over."

"Yep."

"No trips planned or anything?"

"Nothing more exotic than as many Giants games as I can get to. You? Plans for the summer?"

She shrugged. "Not much. Still have some legal and financial ends to tie up, and my other sister's invited me out to her place in Boulder."

"Sweet. I love Boulder."

"Me too. What about . . . Becka is it?"

"Becka."

"What about the two of you?"

"I wish I knew. I'm not a very good boyfriend."

She smiled and shook her head. "Jimmy wasn't either sometimes." She took a sip of her drink. "Husband. Whatever. And I wasn't a very good girlfriend sometimes. Believe me, we had our issues. But in the end, well, I didn't think the end would happen like it did, but in the end, I loved him, really really loved him, and he really really loved me." She shook her head softly. "I just assumed we had another twenty years or more together."

"I'm really sorry," I said.

"Thanks."

We clinked glasses again.

"To love," I said.

"To love." She rolled her lips into each other and nodded.

"I hear it's all you need."

She looked out across the barroom and took another sip of her drink.

— 32 —

The end of a semester is always bittersweet for me. I'm more than ready for it to be over. No more papers to read, classes to prepare for. And I look forward to weeks—months after a spring semester—of freedom. But I'm also always just a little sad, not only about missing the youthful energy and enthusiasm of my students but also knowing that most of them I'll never see or hear from again, though occasionally I'll run into one in the grocery store or get an email asking for a letter of reference. Invariably, too, there are always a handful that I've grown fond of and wish I were able to follow as they take their various paths out into the world.

That Monday night was the last meeting of the semester. Final papers were due. I would grade them, then return them in one-on-one meetings the following week.

A group of five or six students were milling about outside the door as I walked toward the classroom.

They stopped talking when they saw me approaching.

"Well, last class tonight," I said.

They mumbled and shuffled but no one headed inside.

I started to step in past them.

"Mike?" It was Chet Porter. "Are you going to tell us about it?"

Shelly Martin squeezed in through the group. She was wearing black calf-length leggings, a loose-fitting red blouse, and thin white rubber flip-flops, her hair pulled back in a ponytail. She looked like she could have just come from a yoga class. She walked up to her usual seat in the front row, and set her purse, phone, and backpack on the desktop.

"What?" I said.

Porter looked at me quizzically, scowled, and pulled a folded *Independent Journal* out of his back pocket. "Everyone's talking about it," he said, "Like, uh . . . you almost getting killed helping the cops catch that dude."

"You friggin' rock, " Schuyler Nordhof said.

I shrugged. "*Moi*? You must have me confused with someone else."

"Seriously," Nordhof said.

Porter held the newspaper up.

"What is that?" I said. "A *newspaper*? You guys read real *newspapers*?"

"Sometimes," Porter said. "You gonna tell the class about it? Or should we just go to Google's news feed?"

I took a breath and nodded. "Sure. Let's go inside."

I spent the next half hour telling them the story, including how Sarah Rooney'd been waiting outside the classroom that night just a few short weeks ago, which I think made them feel part of the whole thing, as did my explaining why I'd had to cancel class when I'd been in New Mexico. I also told them that Chet Porter's asking whether Johnny Sands might have been gay was a turning point in the case. Shelly Martin gave him a fist-bump.

I passed around a sign-up sheet for next week's meetings.

I turned on the computer and went to YouTube and played "Out on a Limb." I looked at Chet. "You doing okay, dude?"

He nodded, then mouthed the chorus, along with Johnny:

All alone in a tree and out on a limb
Singing my song, hellbound by hymns

"Why don't you pass your papers forward?" I said. "I'll see you next week."

On his way out, Chet stopped at the door, turned, and said, "Hope you like my Johnny Sands paper . . . and, thanks."

Shelley Martin waited until the rest of the class had left, then handed me her paper: "The Ace of Cups—and West Coast Women's Music of the 1960s."

— 33 —

I was waiting for Becka outside the door of her office at San Francisco State when she approached from down the hall, flanked by a couple of young female students, both in ripped skin-tight jeans and black knee-high boots—their thumbs through the straps of their backpacks slung over their shoulders. Becka had on white slacks, a flousy blue blouse, a flower-patterned scarf, and red Converse high-tops. Her glasses were lifted up over her forehead.

She looked great.

She looked away.

She unlocked her office door for her students then followed them inside. "Ten minutes," she said, looking back over her shoulder.

I shrugged. "Take as long as you want." I looked at my watch, then wandered down the hall and looked at the faculty headshots in the glass case outside the department office. Most of them I'd met at various faculty get-togethers, like the annual "Winter Gathering" (*nee* Christmas party), and several different retirement dinners. Nice folks, all of them, and brilliant and highly regarded specialists in their fields but couldn't tell a shortstop from a short-order cook. Although if they ever did go to a baseball game, you can bet they'd be rooting for the left fielder. Both of them.

A sleek, nicely printed postcard below Lawrence Lundford's photo announced the title of his new book, *Culture, Couples, Couplets, Copula, and Conversations: Contextual And Non-Contextual Linguistic Pluralities as Sites of Resistance in the Works of Non-Binary Caribbean Poets of the Mid- to Late-Mid 20th Century.*

I figured I'd wait till the movie came out.

After about fifteen minutes, I walked back down to her office. The door was open. She was sitting behind a desk cluttered with student papers, professional journals, three staplers, two coffee cups with pens and pencils and yellow highlighters sticking up out of them, and her insulated stainless steel water bottle inscribed with black vaguely runic letters that read "Modern Language Association Anglo-Saxon Literature Conference, Kapalua Resort, Maui, Hawaii. 2018."

"What are you doing here?" she said.

Ouch. Not off to good start.

"I was hoping you would read a draft of my *Beowulf* paper."

She almost laughed. "Sit down," she said, indicating a wooden chair in front of a crammed floor-to-ceiling bookshelf.

"Thanks. I didn't really write a paper on *Beowulf*."

"You *didn't*?

"I would, though."

"You would *start* a paper on *Beowulf*."

See "ouch" above. "I follow through on some things," I said. "Most things, in fact."

"Just not interpersonal relationships?" She paused. "Sorry."

"It's okay. Not exactly news."

"So?"

"Want to go to dinner?"

"*Michael* . . . "

"Giants game?"

"Michael!"

"New York?"

"You're getting warmer."

"London?"

She shook her head. "Michael, you know how I feel about you. I love you. A lot. But I'm serious about needing to take a break. Really serious."

I took a breath. "Paris?"

She looked her watch. "I have a department meeting in five minutes. I need to look at some notes."

"Are you guys gonna talk about intentionality and heuristics through a coded critical lens?"

She came closer to laughing. "Unfortunately, probably, yes.

Thankfully, the new contract is on the agenda and there's supposed to be a union rep there."

I stood up. "Okay, then. Guess I'll be on my merry way."

She stood up, too, and walked around the desk. We hugged awkwardly.

"Call me?" I said.

She stepped back and smiled. "Just not . . . "

"Late for dinner," we said together.

I let the door close softly behind me as I headed back down the hall to the parking lot.

— 34 —

It's been a little over a month now since my visit from Howard Silva—M.C. Memphis, Peter Stern, Mr. Meter Reader—and since the last time I saw Becka, though we've talked on the phone a few times. Tonight she's letting me take her to see Emmylou Harris at the Uptown Theater in Napa. She says if it's going to happen at all that she wants to start completely over. I told her that I was good with that.

Yesterday, I sent a down payment to a Newfoundland breeder in Iowa for a little boy from a litter that's due in late July.

Lots of possibilities: Bo, Buddy, Sam, Richie, Domino. Even Johnny.

I'll know when I meet him.

End

Acknowledgements

Thanks to all the friends, family members, teachers, and students over the years who never laughed at my writing. Except when they were supposed to. I'd like to particularly thank Chico State creative writing professors Gary Thompson and Clark Brown (the latter who once signed his novel to me with what I thought said, "Be a writer"; I realized 20 years later that it actually said, "Best wishes," but by then it was too late). Thanks, too, to my daughters Hannah and Gina, both excellent writers themselves, for constantly reminding me what's really important in our lives. And huge thanks to my partner, writer Jan Hill, not only for her love and support but for her finely tuned editor's eye.

Finally, thanks to my old Moon Publications pal Dave Hurst for layout and the front and back cover, and of course to Heidelberg Graphics publisher Larry Jackson.

About the Author

Stephen Metzger has worked as a freelance writer since the early 1980s. He has written numerous travel books and is the co-author of the popular college textbook *The Writer's Way* (Cengage Learning) as well as hundreds of articles and essays for a wide range of local, national, and international publications. He has also published fiction and poetry in literary journals. He taught writing, literature, and journalism at California State University, Chico from 1982 to 2010 and composition at Butte Community College from 2010 to 2018. His daughter Hannah is a seventh-grade science teacher, and his daughter Gina teaches fourth grade, both in Chico. Stephen lives in Chico with his partner, Jan Hill, also a writer, and their sweet but high-maintenance black Lab, Rosie.

www.ingramcontent.com/pod-product-compliance
Lightning Source LLC
Chambersburg PA
CBHW050736250626
47155CB00005B/1796